Going-Out-Of-Religion Sale

Mormons and ex-Mormons, gay and straight, faithful and faithless. In these stories by the author of *Mormon Underwear*, we see Latter-day Saint women organize a sex boycott to force their husbands to grant them the priesthood. Activists dump the bodies of gay suicides on church doorsteps.

A young man fakes his missionary service while living overseas. A devout woman reaches the top tier of heaven but discovers the afterlife isn't quite what she expected. A Mormon advice columnist needs advice of his own. Missionaries in Rome rescue a trafficked woman.

And a young couple sell all their church-related books and artwork at a Going-Out-Of-Religion sale. Sometimes poignant, sometimes amusing, Johnny Townsend's stories look beyond crisp white shirts and freshly baked cookies to reveal the inner secrets of LDS culture.

Praise for Johnny Townsend

In *Zombies for Jesus,* "Townsend isn't writing satire, but deeply emotional and revealing portraits of people who are, with a few exceptions, quite lovable."

Kel Munger, *Sacramento News and Review*

In *Sex among the Saints,* "Townsend writes with a deadpan wit and a supple, realistic prose that's full of psychological empathy….he takes his protagonists' moral struggles seriously and invests them with real emotional resonance."

Kirkus Reviews

Inferno in the French Quarter: The UpStairs Lounge Fire is "a gripping account of all the horrors that transpired that night, as well as a respectful remembrance of the victims."

Terry Firma, Patheos

"Johnny Townsend's 'Partying with St. Roch' [in the anthology *Latter-Gay Saints*] tells a beautiful, haunting tale."

Kent Brintnall, Out in Print: Queer Book Reviews

Selling the City of Enoch is "sharply intelligent…pleasingly complex…The stories are full of…doubters, but there's no vindictiveness in these pages; the characters continuously poke holes in Mormonism's more extravagant absurdities, but they take very little pleasure in doing so….Many of Townsend's stories…have a provocative edge to them, but this [book] displays a great deal of insight as well…a playful, biting and surprisingly warm collection."

Kirkus Reviews

Gayrabian Nights is "an allegorical tour de force…a hard-core emotional punch."

Gay. Guy. Reading and Friends

The Washing of Brains has "A lovely writing style, and each story [is] full of unique, engaging characters….immensely entertaining."

Rainbow Awards

In *Dead Mankind Walking*, "Townsend writes in an energetic prose that balances crankiness and humor….A rambunctious volume of short, well-crafted essays…"

Kirkus Reviews

Going-Out-Of-Religion Sale

Johnny Townsend

Contents

Woman on the Wharf

"Anziano, we need to find a Golden Contact tonight." Elder Allred sat on the edge of his cot and wagged his finger at me. Every time he did it, I thought of my mother. "We haven't taught a single lesson in two weeks. I can't take being called out at district meetings anymore."

"Feel free to be inspired," I returned.

"You're the senior companion, Anziano Mortensen," Allred said. "It's your responsibility." He pouted and I reflected again on how effeminate he sometimes looked. I caught him looking at pretty girls often enough and didn't think he was gay. My friend Barry from college could effectively pass for straight, and I wondered if people like Elder Allred ever tried to pass for gay.

"You're just going to let me lead you down the path to hell without putting out any resistance?" I replied. "If a wife is an equal partner to her husband, surely you have to take *some* responsibility in our companionship."

Elder Allred frowned, paused a long moment, and repeated, "We need to find a Golden Contact tonight." The expression on his face at that moment would probably fail to attract either a man or a woman. But then, the look of smugness on my own probably wasn't especially attractive either.

Our lunch period was almost over, and we'd have to leave our apartment at 3:30. Ostia was a small town, so there weren't many areas we hadn't already tried out. Italians this close to Rome weren't particularly interested in Mormonism. But my companion was right. As missionaries of the One True Church, we had an obligation to bring as many souls as possible to the gospel.

I'd been out fourteen months while Elder Allred had been out five. We'd been together here in Ostia just over five weeks. It was the spring of 1993, and I had no idea my life was about to change forever.

"Let's do some Spirit Tracting down by the waterfront," I suggested. This was a tactic missionaries sometimes used when their assigned tracting areas weren't producing many investigators. We'd take a break from our routine for one night, going instead where the Spirit led us, and try to find someone who'd been praying for the Lord to send us their way.

Elder Allred smiled. "Cool! The waterfront's always fun."

We put on our suit jackets, grabbed our flip charts, and stood by the door with our heads bowed as I offered a companionship prayer. Then we headed down the stairs to the street. A few people glanced our way as we walked along the sidewalk, but most had learned long ago not to make eye contact. When I'd first arrived in Italy, I'd felt special. Our polyester suits and white shirts seemed to scream "American!" and I could tell everyone was jealous.

Sometimes, I felt like a spy, the fantasy nourished by the fact that our mission leader, President Holland, had worked for the FBI most of his adult life. But as time went on, I began to feel more like one of the Three Nephites, so ignored while preaching I could remain unnoticed for two thousand years. Lately, I'd begun feeling like a simple salesman. One who wasn't making much on commission.

It hadn't helped that my previous companion, Elder Becker, had disappeared one night while I slept, made his way to the nearby Fiumicino airport, and flown home without a word to anyone. Now I could hardly stop thinking about Orem. And Janine.

But Janine would never marry me if I came home early from my mission. Only an RM for good Mormon girls. Ten months longer wasn't forever. I could make it.

"Buon giorno," I said to a man waiting at a bus stop. He looked at me nervously and turned away. "We're representatives of The Church of Jesus Christ of Latter-day Saints," I went on. "Ami i tuoi figli?" Do you love your children? We could use the "tu" with men.

The man glanced at me worriedly again, his eyes darting in every direction. I'd seen the expression a thousand times. He clearly wasn't going to answer without further prodding, so I continued. "We know a way you can be with your family forever. What's the best time we can meet to talk more about this?"

The man closed his eyes, steeled himself, and looked up the street for the bus, which was nowhere in sight. But he was no longer part of the conversation. I tapped Elder Allred on the shoulder and we continued along the sidewalk.

I'd had companions who criticized every failed approach, but Elder Allred knew the stats, the number of approaches one had to make even to get a lukewarm response. A block later, he nodded at a middle-aged woman with a tinge of gray and started talking. It was against mission rules for elders to approach women or for sister missionaries to approach men. I didn't stop my companion, though, since he was at least making an attempt.

The woman muttered, "Sono cattolica," shook her head, and kept walking.

We continued with the "24-hour work" for another couple of hours. Then I pointed to a corner bar, and Elder Allred and I darted in to order some acqua minerale. It was a chance to sit for a few minutes. I wanted to ask my companion his plans after college. I wanted to ask what his favorite movie was. If he liked jazz.

But we weren't supposed to talk about anything that didn't promote the work. From the way he fingered his missionary haircut in the mornings, I could assume he didn't like short hair, but he never actually said anything about it. I'd mentioned Janine a couple of times, but I had no idea if Allred had a girlfriend back home himself. I didn't even know Elder Allred's first name.

"Come on, Elder," I said. "Time to start feeling the Spirit."

"You're supposed to always speak Italian," he said, wagging his finger.

I nodded and we continued on toward the waterfront, stopping when we reached Via dell'Idroscalo. Most of the buildings in the area looked to have been built in the 1930's, though I was no expert. Anything that recent was considered "new." When I'd been stationed in Napoli earlier in my mission, our building had been constructed sometime in the mid-1800's. Even that was considered relatively new.

The apartment I shared with Elder Allred, though, couldn't be more than fifteen or twenty years old. While we saw occasional new construction, there wasn't really much need for it. Bishop Cuccia from the Trionfale Ward had given a talk once about how the birth rate in Italy had been decreasing steadily for years, and the only way to maintain the population was to allow immigrants into the country. The most noticeable were all the Africans, though it seemed likely there'd been at least some Italians with African ancestry for the past two thousand years. One of the de Medicis was black.

Bishop Cuccia thought a better solution than new immigration would be Italian women bearing more children again, the way Heavenly Father intended. If Catholics had given up on large families, it was time for Mormons to take over the task.

Elder Allred and I knocked on doors from just before six until a few minutes past eight. Not a single person let us in. It was always a risk to go Spirit Tracting, of course, since the lack of success proved beyond a shadow of a doubt one wasn't in tune with the Holy Ghost. The same thing had happened last time we tried it, and Elder Allred had asked sarcastically, "What spirit are you following?"

I'd replied, "Don't blame me. Maybe there's some sort of sexual sin in your past. Have you been masturbating lately?"

Elder Allred had shut up immediately. I noticed he was holding his tongue tonight, probably preemptively. I hated being a jerk, but I hated being constantly criticized even more. My father kept asking when I was going to be promoted to district leader and then zone leader. Anything less would be a stain on his honor. He'd given up on my becoming Assistant to the President, but he still held out for ZL.

Meanwhile, Janine was asking how much longer it would take before I baptized my twentieth convert. For some reason, that was the magical number for her. She continually hinted we might not be able to resume dating if I didn't reach it.

Since the average number of baptisms per missionary in the Rome mission was three, and I'd only baptized one so far, I understood I might need to start looking for a new girlfriend once I returned home.

When I'd written something to Mom about the relationship feeling a bit transactional, she wrote back immediately that couples didn't always marry for love.

"What you want," she said, "is someone who will help you become a god."

President Holland and the AP's were also constantly on everyone's case about not baptizing. One elder who'd been out twenty-three months was sent home early because he'd never baptized a single person. The mission president thought he had a "bad attitude" and therefore didn't deserve to finish his mission honorably.

Even my friend Barry back at the U kept asking me, "When are you going to do something useful on your mission?" He thought I should be feeding the homeless every day.

"We're giving people the bread of life," I told him. "What could possibly be more important?"

As time went on, though, I couldn't help but wonder if feeding a few converts whatever amount of spiritual sustenance we could provide was in any way equal to feeding some actual, real food to the dozens or hundreds of *disoccupati* and *senzatetto* we saw every day.

Perhaps I'd ask President Holland about it at our next zone conference. He hadn't liked my idea to allow missionaries to donate plasma. We weren't allowed to donate blood because it would "weaken" us, but donating plasma would carry no such risk.

"You let *us* worry about what's appropriate," Holland had told me. "Just follow the rules we give you."

"Elder Allred," I said, "let's walk along the waterfront for a while and see what happens."

He nodded and we walked the rest of the way to the water. There were docks and wharfs and boats and several laborers and seamen. None of the men looked approachable. I didn't want to be thrown into the ocean by some guy we might annoy. But there were a few women in the area, too. Most of them seemed lost, just standing around, looking about listlessly. Perhaps they were waiting for their boyfriends due in soon on whatever boats they worked aboard.

Elder Allred grabbed my arm. "Let's go talk to her," he said, pointing to a lone figure staring down into the water from a wharf. This woman was not middle-aged, probably only a few years older than we were, so it would definitely seem inappropriate to any judgmental eyes looking our way. But I was tired of doing approaches, and if Elder Allred was willing to try one, I wasn't going to stop him.

As we came closer, I could see the woman tense, but she put on a brave smile. I realized she was probably afraid of being mugged, even if we were wearing suits. Sister missionaries always had to be back in their apartments a full hour before the elders every evening. Italian macho could become a little threatening at night. Once when a former companion and I got caught out late in the Napoli ghetto, I'd felt rather threatened myself.

"Buona sera," Elder Allred said with a big smile. "Come sta?" We had to use the "lei" with women.

"You speak English?" the woman replied with a strong accent.

People often tried to practice the language with us. Especially little kids asking, "What taim eez eet?"

"Yes," Elder Allred told her. "We're missionaries with—"

"You can to help me?" she went on, her thick accent making it difficult to understand. Both hands were outstretched in front of her, palms up. This seemed an odd time and place to be begging, and she didn't really look poor, though perhaps a little tarty, now that I saw her up close.

"What's up?" I asked, feeling I'd better take over the conversation.

The woman put her hand on my arm, and I couldn't help but feel a tiny thrill at the touch. Shaking hands with other missionaries and church members didn't fill all my sensory needs. "My name Loredana Lupei," she struggled. "You can to say that?"

"Loredana Lupei," I repeated. She sighed to hear her name.

"I take job as housekeeper," she continued, "but when I arrive Italy, Signor Santi take the passport. I am trap-ped working here all the nights. He does not to let me leave. You must to help me. Please."

"Working?" Elder Allred looked confused.

Thick as I often was, I finally realized what was going on. "Can you come home with us?" I asked. "Or do you bring men to your place?"

"Anziano!"

Perhaps he wasn't as slow as I thought.

"I—I must to stay here," she said. Her eyes flitted about nervously. It was the same trapped expression I saw every day when I stopped people on the street. Only the look of fear on this woman's face was far stronger. I noticed what appeared to be a bruise on her left forearm, almost hidden with make-up.

"Are you here every night, or do you work different areas?"

"This place where I am work."

Elder Allred looked from Loredana's face to mine and back to hers again in horror.

"We'll talk to our mission president," I said, "and we'll be back tomorrow night." I made sure to catch her eye. "Tomorrow night," I repeated.

I turned and grabbed my companion's arm, and we hurried all the way back to our apartment. It was almost 9:00 when I sat on my bed next to the telephone.

"Hello?" asked President Holland when he picked up in the mission home.

I wasted no time explaining the situation with the Romanian woman and asked if he could get us help immediately with his government connections. Elder Allred sat on his bed watching me, his mouth hanging open. Mormon chivalry was welling up inside me. I was doing something useful for the first time on my mission, perhaps the first time in my life.

"Elder Mortensen," President Holland answered crisply, "you need to report to my office first thing in the morning, and we'll see about doing an emergency transfer and demoting you back to junior companion."

Did I hear him correctly? "This isn't about me," I said. "It's about Loredana."

"You're on a first-name basis with a *puttana*?"

Odd that he struggled in every meeting with the language and yet knew that word.

"You are expressly forbidden to talk to strange women," the president continued in a cool tone. "This is a local police problem, not ours. How would it look if it became known two Mormon missionaries were talking to a prostitute?" He breathed out heavily in disgust.

"But President—"

"We don't get involved in things like this," he went on. "Bad publicity hurts the work."

"But—"

"See me first thing in the morning," he repeated. "And you'd damn well better be fasting." There was a click as the mission president hung up the phone.

Did I mention I was thick?

Elder Allred and I sat on our beds looking at each other in silence. "He's not going to help?" he finally asked, pouting.

I again noticed how effeminate he looked, and an idea began to form. I explained what I was thinking, and while my companion looked horrified at first, he was soon helping me formulate our plan. We made our way back to the waterfront, but Loredana was nowhere in sight. I wasn't sure what her work hours were, but we decided to wait a little, and twenty minutes later, she walked back to her spot. I grabbed my companion's arm and we went out to meet her again. She smiled weakly at seeing us, nervous but hopeful.

"We talked to our mission president," I said.

"He will to help?"

I shook my head and the woman winced as if she'd been slapped.

"But *we* will," I went on quickly.

"You—you can do what?" Her eyes darted about.

"You're coming back with us to our apartment," I told her.

Her eyes narrowed immediately and she stepped backward.

"You're about the same size as Elder Allred here," I explained. "We'll cut your hair, you'll put on his suit, you'll use his passport, and we're flying to the States on the first available flight."

Loredana's mouth fell open. She needed some dental work.

"I should have just enough money on my emergency credit card to pay for our tickets."

"I do not understand."

"The mission president may not care about helping you find your passport, but he won't have any choice but to help

Elder Allred get a new one." I suddenly remembered with a shudder my cousin Zack who'd served a mission to Brazil. His mission president had kept all the missionary passports in a safe at the mission home. I reached for Loredana's hand.

She still looked confused. "I do not understand," she said again.

Fair enough, since she'd be "illegal" in the States without her own passport.

"We don't have any time to waste," I said. "Let's go."

We hurried back along the dark streets, looking over our shoulders to make sure we weren't being followed. Elder Allred got out the scissors, laid a spare suit in the bathroom, and we ushered Loredana in to wash off her make-up. She either liked the warm water or felt especially dirty because we heard the water running for a long, long time. I finally knocked on the door.

"We need to get moving," I said.

Elder Allred gave me a kiss when Loredana and I left the apartment around midnight, and I never saw him again.

As it turned out, getting to America was the easy part. There was lots of misery and grief that followed. But Loredana finally got her passport, she eventually got a green card after we married several months later, and we moved to San Francisco shortly after I graduated from the University of Utah. I found a job straight off with REST, Real Escape from the Sex Trade, and began doing what I could to fight trafficking in America. The scope of the problem was far beyond anything I had imagined.

I never set foot in a Mormon church again, and most of my family haven't spoken to me in years. But I don't regret my time as a Mormon missionary for one minute.

These days, I get my spiritual satisfaction in other ways. Loredana and I go down to the waterfront and feed the homeless on weekends. She's a bank branch manager during the day, a mother to our two girls at all times, and gives a public lecture on trafficking about once a month. We've gone back to Rome, visited her family in Bucharest, and toured a few other world capitals. But everywhere we go, as we look at the beauty of the local attractions, we're always aware what's happening just two or three blocks away.

Once, in London, we were stopped by two Mormon missionaries in Soho. "What do you know about the Mormon Church?" one of them asked, smiling eagerly. It wasn't until that very moment, when I saw the dull look in his eyes behind the dazzling smile, that I realized my wife had helped me escape imprisonment as well.

I wondered whatever became of poor Elder Allred.

I squeezed Loredana's hand, nodded to our young teens beside us, and we walked on.

Kidnapping Jeremy

"What if it doesn't work, Cal?" Allison squeezed my hand.

"If we can't save him now, it's only going to get harder later," I replied. "At least he already hates his mission."

"Yes, but he also believes *he's* the one at fault, not the mission leaders or the Church. He's always trying to 'repent' and do better."

I took another sip of my ginger ale, watching my wife tear the plastic of her empty peanut package into shreds.

"Allison," I said, leaning over so that our heads touched, "we've already lost Darren and Elizabeth. We don't have any choice if we want to save Jeremy."

Allison squeezed my hand again, but with her free hand, she wiped away a tear. At least she no longer sobbed. It was hearing her in the bathroom night after night that had forced me to come up with a plan.

"There's nothing more we can do while we're on the plane," I said. "Let's just relax and watch the movie."

Allison nodded bravely and we put in our ear buds. *Suffragette* was playing, not the cheeriest movie in the world, but watching someone else's struggle put our own in perspective. When we'd told our oldest son, Darren, that we'd learned too much about Church history to believe any longer, rather than ask us what we'd discovered, he told us never to contact him again.

We quickly called Elizabeth, still in her last year at Brigham Young, and while she initially seemed open to maintaining a relationship, the following day she called back and said "someone" had told her that talking to us any longer would endanger her continued enrollment at the university.

By the time we emailed Jeremy on his mission in New Orleans, both his siblings had already warned him. He responded to our email the way he was trained. "Satan always attacks the best missionaries any way he can." He asked or, rather, *told* us to stop emailing him.

It was laughable really. I was paying for his mission. Jeremy had saved up less than $1500 on his own ahead of time, and he was in the ninth month of his mission, so his funds had long since run out. I could simply stop paying. But that would do nothing to salvage our relationship.

For that matter, I wasn't sure kidnapping him from his missionary apartment and forcing him into deprogramming would help, either.

Before long, the plane landed in Dallas. After a half hour layover, we continued on our way to New Orleans. We stopped at Hertz to pick up our rental car and then drove the rest of the way to our hotel on St. Charles Avenue. It was way too expensive for our moderate means, but it was the closest we could get to Jeremy's apartment Uptown.

"Let's go get him now," Allison said as soon as we checked in.

"We haven't even unpacked yet."

"I don't want to unpack. I want to get our boy and get out of here."

I shook my head. "Let me call Fletcher first." Fletcher was the liaison with Dr. Haysworth, the psychologist who would help deprogram Jeremy. He'd drive the car after we grabbed Jeremy, and together, we'd take him to a location in the suburbs where Jeremy would spend a week, or two, or three, being deprogrammed. I'd taken out an equity loan on the house to pay for the whole thing. I wasn't quite sure of the legality, of course. After all, Jeremy was over eighteen. But given that he'd still been living at home until the day he left for his mission, and given that he'd need to return home at least temporarily after his mission, I was willing to take whatever legal risk was required. If the deprogramming was successful, it was unlikely Jeremy would press any charges.

I called Fletcher on my cell, and we arranged to meet in an hour and drive the remaining several blocks to Jeremy's neighborhood.

"Oh, Cal, I can't stand it," said Allison. "I want to go get him *now*."

I held both her hands. "He may hate us for the rest of his life."

Allison sniffed. "He already hates us. What do we have to lose?" She looked into my eyes. "Oh, Cal, we *have* to save at least one of them! They're all worried about being a family for 'eternity.' I'm worried about *now*."

With the Internet out there, and the increasingly severe doctrines of the Church, our kids might very well end up leaving on their own, if we gave them time. But Darren already had a good job right out of college, and it was unbearable to realize he was paying so much to the Church every month in tithing, supporting that oppressive institution. The longer Elizabeth stayed at BYU, the more she was being indoctrinated every day, making it that much harder to think for herself. And the more likely she'd be married in the temple to another devout member, making things even worse. What if it took her fifteen more years to see the truth? After all, it took Allison and me a lot longer than that. We couldn't bear to miss out on so much of our kids' lives.

And Jeremy. Not only being indoctrinated but spending every moment indoctrinating others as well. Far more members who'd served missions stayed in the Church than their counterparts who'd never gone. Missions were much more about converting the missionary than they were about baptizing new members.

Just after 4:00, Fletcher knocked on our hotel room door. We all shook hands grimly, and then he nodded for us to follow. We drove several blocks down Napoleon, passing Magazine and parking on Annunciation. "How close are we?" I asked as we climbed out of the car.

"Tchoupitoulas is the next street over," Fletcher replied, lighting up a cigarette. I caught myself frowning. Not everything about the Church was bad. It was his life, though, so I didn't say anything.

"Tchoupitoulas," I repeated. It was the first time I'd heard the word pronounced aloud.

"You guys will station yourselves a few doors down from Jeremy's apartment," Fletcher went on. "You'll push this button"—he pointed to a tiny device in his hand—"and I'll drive right up. We need to do this before he gets inside the door, so be on your toes."

"Oh my God," Allison breathed.

I wanted to pray and ask for Heavenly Father's help and protection. Instead, I took Allison's hands again and squeezed. She looked at me and forced a smile. We nodded at Fletcher and headed toward the river. The area was pretty run down, but that was to be expected. Paint was peeling on many of the wooden structures. Yards were overgrown. Trash skipped along the sidewalk in the light breeze. It was only April, but the air was already hot and humid. "Sultry," as Anne Ramsey would say.

Would this kidnapping end up as a funny family story one day?

"What's that smell?" asked Allison.

I shook my head and pointed for us to keep going. We turned the corner and quickly surveyed our surroundings. No young men in white shirts and ties. We'd used Street View to determine ahead of time where we could loiter while waiting for Jeremy and his companion to show up. Now I saw that the large bush we'd hoped to hide behind had been trimmed. Great, I thought, the one person in the neighborhood who kept up their property. We walked one house farther down than we'd planned and sat on someone's cracked front steps, just inches from the sidewalk. An eighteen-wheeler rumbled by on its way to a nearby wharf.

"There are a lot of black people around here," Allison noted, her voice wavering slightly.

We clearly needed a bit of deprogramming ourselves. We'd been doing the best we could these past few months, but it was hard to overcome a lifetime of lies and misinformation. "What if Jeremy falls back into the Church after we rescue him?" I asked. "We'll still be in Salt Lake, after all. Even at the University of Utah, there'll be Mormons everywhere."

"But he's a smart boy," Allison said. "He won't go back."

I'd been watching people leave our congregation for quite some time. Like most Mormons, my reaction had been to dig in and try to avoid exposing myself to "Satan's lies." I knew four couples from our ward who had left the Church, and either the husband or the wife in two of those pairs had ended up going back to the Church after only a few years. I wondered if there was any research on recidivism among those who escaped cults. Certainly, no one went back because they believed again. Of that I was sure. They always went back because of "feelings." For "family."

I wondered if we were doing the right thing. Were we so special *we* couldn't be deceived?

Stop it!

An hour passed. Then another. It was beginning to grow dark when I felt Allison's nails in my wrist. I looked up the street. There they were. I pushed the button for Fletcher, and Allison started to stand, but I held her back. "Not yet," I said.

I wanted the car ready at the curb. Fletcher would have a hypodermic ready once we hustled our son into the back seat.

Allison pulled away and started walking quickly toward the missionaries. I stood up and followed. "Jeremy?" Allison called.

The missionaries stopped, Jeremy staring at us in shock from twenty feet away. "Mom? Dad? What are you doing here?"

Where was that car?

"Jeremy! We're coming to rescue you!" Allison held out her arms and started running toward our son.

Jeremy's companion tried to step in front of him, but Jeremy held him back and thrust his right arm upward, holding it to the square. "I command you in the name of Jesus Christ to stop where you are!" he demanded. We were both so shocked we froze in our tracks. Our son was using the priesthood to stop *us*?

Maybe he was too far gone already.

"Jeremy…" I said.

"It's Elder Hawks," he corrected me.

"Elder Hawks," I said, stifling the nausea I felt, "just spend a couple of weeks with us. If you still want to come back after that, you can." If he was willing to pay his own way the next fifteen months. And I'd certainly never provide the tuition for BYU. We'd pry him loose one way or the other.

"Dad," Jeremy said calmly, "you're a High Priest. You served a mission to Mexico. You were a temple worker." He paused. "You *know* what you felt. You *know* the Church is true. You can't deny it."

Oh my God. He was trying to reconvert us. I kept hearing Priesthood lessons. Conference talks. The voices of bishops and stake presidents.

Where was that goddamn car?

"Mom," Jeremy went on, "you were the Relief Society president. You taught Gospel Doctrine—"

"Come with us right this minute, young man!" Allison ordered.

"In the name of Jesus Christ…" Jeremy began. Right at that moment, Fletcher came careening around the corner. The fool must have been taking a smoke break and was now trying to make up time once he realized we'd pressed the button to summon him. But the idiot was coming from the wrong direction. Now he'd have to cross into the oncoming lane to get to the curb. And—

An eighteen-wheeler struck the rear corner of the car just as Fletcher was pulling to the curb, spinning it out of control. "Allison!" I yelled. I reached to grab her but she was still several feet ahead of me. The car knocked her off the sidewalk and into the house with the trimmed bush. She slumped over the trunk of the car.

"Oh, Jesus!" I ran over to her, and Fletcher jumped out of the car, holding his head. "Back up!" I shouted. "Back up!" Fletcher slid back into the car and put it in reverse.

Allison crumpled to the ground. I reached down to feel her pulse. It was still there. "Call 9-1-1!" I said.

Fletcher shook his head. "Touro is just a few blocks away. Let's get her in the car."

"Jeremy," I began, but when I looked for him, I found that both he and his companion were gone.

Fletcher and I managed to get Allison to the emergency room, probably injuring her more in the process. She spent the night in ICU while I ended up in the Orleans Parish jail, charged with "conspiracy" to kidnap my son. But the next morning, I had a visitor.

"I gave Mom a blessing," Jeremy told me. "She's going to be okay."

I looked into my son's face, so bold and confident. So calm and assured. I felt an invisible hand squeezing my chest. Had God actually intervened, I wondered? What if I was wrong? What if Allison and I were both mistaken?

I shook my head. No, no, no, I told myself. No, no, no!

Quicksand.

"Dad," Jeremy said softly, "I can help you." He paused. "Let the Spirit back into your heart. I beg you in the name of Jesus Christ." His companion looked ahead blandly.

What if I lost Allison, I thought. I stared at my youngest son. What if I lost all three of my children? What if I lost *everything*?

"Elder Hawks," I said miserably, "will you teach me?" I swallowed. "Bear your testimony to me. I—I want to believe again." I could be my son's first missionary baptism. I closed my eyes for a moment, but I couldn't pray.

Jeremy smiled sweetly at me and opened his Bible.

May God Strike Me Dead

I admit it. I'm an asshole. I've always been this way, since the time I told my dad at the dinner table that yes, I'd heard him fart, to the time I told my mom when she was lecturing me against masturbating that I'd already found her vibrator and used it myself.

Like I said, I'm an asshole.

The only real problem during the latter incident was that my nose started to bleed right after my smart comment. I got nose bleeds any time I felt especially nervous or excited. It happened a couple of times in the principal's office, too, and once in a Personal Priesthood interview.

Some people blushed. I bled.

My attitude only got worse as I grew older. As a priest, I'd deliberately misread the sacrament prayer card so I'd have to repeat it over and over and over, until finally the bishop would march to the sacrament table and just order us to get on with it. On my mission, I even talked one investigator into a fake baptism. He'd already told me he had no intention of ever joining the Church, that he'd simply wanted to learn a little about us.

But when my companion was off in the bathroom, I quickly enlisted Angel in my stunt. He was a bit of a jerk, too. We decided I would start to submerge him but never get him fully under the surface. Just like with the sacrament prayer, I ended up dunking him five times, his left hand always remaining above the water, until finally, as prearranged, he ran out of the font and through the rear doors of the building screaming.

Need I point out that I'm thirty-two now and still unmarried?

I'm an asshole.

I've made an effort to restrain myself for the last six months at my new job and came close to going on a date with one of my coworkers last week. Jenny and I and the rest of the department were in our weekly business meeting when our manager tried something new to inspire us. "I'm going to give you a writing prompt," Suzanne said. "When I say 'go,' start writing the first thing that comes to your mind and don't stop until I tell you to. Write about your deepest, darkest fear in the world. Now 'go.'"

Everyone wrote for five minutes, and then Suzanne raised her hand. "Okay, everyone pair up with the coworker next to you and share what you've written."

I was appalled that I was supposed to share my deepest fears with anyone, much less with a person chosen at random, but Jenny crossed the room and stood next to me, even though I wasn't officially "next" to her in our business meeting circle. I smiled, since I'd often thought about asking her to dinner and had only held off because I figured I'd end up ruining our working relationship instead.

Jenny handed her paper to me with a shy smile. She wrote that her biggest fear was never being truly loved, and if she were, that she'd never really believe it and so would still feel all alone her whole life.

"I think that's something many of us feel," I said when I finished reading. "Though I find it hard to believe you aren't already loved by many people."

So maybe I'm not *always* an asshole. Just most of the time.

Jenny smiled and grabbed my paper. She looked at it, looked at me, and began laughing uproariously. I'd followed Jack Nicholson's lead and written "All work and no play makes Damien a dull boy" over and over and over.

I took that as approval and worked up the nerve I needed. "Want to go out this weekend?" I smiled.

"You are out of your cotton-picking mind," she replied, still laughing but serious. "Maybe there *are* worse things than being alone."

Bitch.

After the meeting, Suzanne called me into her office. "Damien," she said, "you're continually a disruptive force in this office."

"I don't mean to be," I returned as sweetly as possible.

She closed her eyes. "I know you were the one who put that book on my chair," she continued. "I've had IT install cameras in the department now, so I'll catch you next time you try something like that."

I cocked my head to illustrate my confusion. Suzanne shook hers in return. "You're not fooling anyone, mister. I only keep you here because you do good work. But you need to watch yourself."

I of course knew perfectly well what she was talking about. A couple of months back, Suzanne had confessed to starting *No Man Knows My History*. She was LDS, as was half the staff in our company. "After only two chapters," she told me, "I knew the book was written by the Devil, and I threw it in the lake." It was clear she was warning me against delving too deeply into the mysteries, knowing I sometimes talked with the others about things I read online. "That book was downright Satanic."

I waited three days and then bought another copy of the book in a used book store. I came in early one day, dunked the book in the bathroom sink, and then placed it on her office chair.

So I guess I cost the company money when they had to install the security cameras. But I was no fool. I was already looking for another job.

The thing is, I really wanted to go out with Jenny. So ever since our writing prompt, I'd made a greater effort to be pleasant around her. I brought her a Diet 7-Up when I went on break. I bought us both bananas as snacks. I carried her recycling and compost down the hall for her. I volunteered for a project I knew she didn't want to do herself.

This morning, I saw her giving me an odd look, as if she might be reevaluating. I knew I needed to make a significant change in my personality unless I wanted Jenny's fear to be my reality. So just before closing, I went over to her desk.

"Hey," I said.

"Yes?"

"I was wondering if you'd like to come to my apartment this Saturday night." Her mouth opened in astonishment and I quickly continued. "You can bring a friend, male or female. It's not a date. I just thought you might like to watch my DVD of *Going Clear*. We can make fun of Scientologists together." Jenny was LDS, too, of course.

Jenny frowned. Then her eyes narrowed and she shook her head. "I know you far too well, Damien. You're just going to point out how Mormons are so much like Scientologists. You're trying to lead me to apostasy."

I came close to saying, "No, I'm just trying to lead you to my bed." And frankly, I was happy to invite along whoever she might bring with her this Saturday as well.

But I took a deep breath and tried to formulate a calmer response. Unfortunately, that deep breath, along with the tension of the moment, set off the inner workings of my nose again. I knew I had only a few seconds before the blood started flowing out full force.

So I smiled my most innocent smile and said, "Jenny, if I have any plans to lead you astray, may God strike me dead right now." I leaned over her desk so the blood would splatter there and not on my shirt. I aimed for a report she was working on.

Suzanne didn't even ask why Jenny was screaming. She just called Security and had me escorted right out of the office. I didn't even get to go back to my desk to grab my banana.

I need a job where being an asshole isn't a problem. And I need a change of scenery. There's a certain megacompany in the Seattle area where I might apply.

I wonder if I could ask Suzanne for a reference.

Bishops Move Diagonally

Detective Carter peered down at the body in front of him. The plump, middle-aged man lay on the floor beside his chair. There was no window in the office. No one outside could have seen in. The man was wearing a suit and tie, fouled a little, whatever he'd just been eating having been regurgitated at the last moment. The detective saw a plate of cookies still on the desk next to some papers. Perhaps from a Relief Society sister. Carter's wife was always bringing treats to their own bishop.

"Bag the cookies," Carter ordered a young man on the forensics team. "And bag the vomit." Those and the body would all be tested for poisons, among other things. He needed to solve this case if he wanted the raise he'd been asking for every month for the past half year.

Captain Jeffries kept saying there weren't enough murders in the Valley to warrant a raise, but Carter had replied that keeping murders down was reason enough to grant one. This was a chance to earn money on the captain's terms. Detective Carter browsed among the other items on the desk. There was an agenda with several appointments listed, including two earlier this evening. He pointed at the book, motioning for his partner, Det. Andreason, to take a look.

"Can you get me the addresses of these folks, Mr. Templeton?" Det. Andreason asked, turning to the man who'd called the police half an hour ago. Andreason was older than Carter by a decade but still his junior, something Carter knew she wasn't happy about. She was a non-member, which probably explained why she never seemed to understand most of the city she was trying to investigate. She acted as if Mormons were like everyone else, a serious miscalculation.

"None of our church members would have done this!" Templeton exclaimed. He was in his mid-thirties, balding but reasonably fit. Carter was roughly the same age and build, but *he* had hair, he noted with a grim smile.

"We didn't say they had," Carter returned. "But they may know something. Might have seen something. Your bishop may have said something in passing to them that we need to know." He paused, noting Andreason's look of irritation. "Did Mr. Grigg tell you who had given him the cookies?" In secular investigations, Carter always used non-LDS terminology. Sometimes, it helped root out the killer, and sometimes, it made things more difficult.

"No one would poison Bishop Grigg!" Templeton insisted.

"It's entirely possible Mr. Grigg had a stroke or aneurysm," Andreason said soothingly, trying to take over again, "but we have to follow every possibility until the autopsy and toxicology reports are complete."

Carter knew that some drugs might not show up for several days, but they couldn't wait till every last result was in before starting to investigate. "You yourself said you thought he was poisoned when you called. Are you changing your story?" He held his pen over his notebook, ready to write.

"Oh, my…my *heck*!" Templeton said, groaning.

Carter took photos of all the appointments from the last several days in the agenda, plus those of the upcoming days. The young man on the forensics team bagged the book, and Carter had Templeton give him contact information for each of the names. This took surprisingly little time, as Templeton seemed to have access to all of this at his fingertips.

It was almost 9:00 by this point, perhaps too late to be knocking on doors, but it wasn't often a Mormon bishop was murdered in Salt Lake. Just for PR purposes, if not his own curiosity, Det. Carter wanted to act immediately. The sooner he wrapped this up, the more likely he'd get that raise.

"Is Mrs. Caldwell in?" Carter asked when a man about thirty answered his knock a few minutes later. It hadn't taken long to arrive at the first house. In this part of Mt. Olympus, it seemed that most of Mr. Grigg's congregation all resided within a ten-block radius.

"What's this about?" asked Mr. Caldwell.

"Nelson Grigg has died," Det. Andreason said softly, taking a step forward, "and we want to talk to everyone who saw him the past couple of days. It appears your wife talked to him earlier this evening?"

"Bishop Grigg!" the man breathed. "No!" He frowned. "Well, I don't know anything about my wife meeting with him. Becca, did you talk to the bishop today?"

A timid woman with dark brown hair walked up next to her husband. "Yes, I talked to the bishop," she said quietly. "What happened? Did he have a heart attack? He didn't seem to look well."

Detectives Carter and Andreason looked quickly at each other. Was this reliable information, or was Becca trying to build a competing narrative? Carter decided to let his partner pursue the questioning. He would get points for training, too. Andreason asked if they could come inside, and they all sat in the living room. But Becca looked reluctant to speak.

"We have to know what you two were talking about," said Det. Andreason, continuing in her soft voice. She always tried to use that technique when she thought it made her seem less threatening. In Carter's experience, it was better to be threatening. "We need to know anything Mr. Grigg might have said."

Becca looked nervously at her husband. "Honey…"

"Go on," he said, "tell the police what you talked about. *I* want to know what you talked about, too."

"Honey…"

"Go on."

"Sweetie, I need to talk to the police alone." She looked thinner and smaller as she said it, but her tone was firm. Her husband's eyebrows furrowed, his lips set rather firmly, but he stood and left the room. Mrs. Caldwell breathed out heavily.

"We'll try to be as discreet as possible," Det. Carter said. Andreason held up a hand toward him to indicate she was going to be the one directing the conversation.

"What were you meeting about?" she asked, almost in a whisper. Women.

"Jake and I have a one-year-old," Becca replied, just as softly. "He wants to start trying for a second child, but I don't want any more. I…" She looked down the hallway to make sure her husband wasn't close enough to overhear. "I asked Bishop Grigg if Heavenly Father would be upset with me if I had my tubes tied." She covered her face in her hands but then looked up at the detectives again. "He said it was okay, that Heavenly Father understood. But…but do you think God struck him down for saying that?"

Carter's gut instinct told him the woman was telling the truth, but he let Andreason finish the interview. She needed the practice. She still routinely tried to ferret things out, always a risk. Better to just get an overall feel for what was happening and go with that. It had never failed him yet. Det. Andreason was thorough, however, and managed to pull one more interesting comment out of the woman.

"Bishop Grigg has been a different man the past few months. Ever since the new policy banning kids of gay couples from getting baptized. He spoke out in church about it once and got a lot of flak. Some of the other members are hoping he'll be replaced." She paused. "Well, I guess he *will* be replaced now."

Back in the car, Det. Carter turned to his partner. "What are your thoughts, Andreason?"

"Could be anyone in that congregation, if he was really starting to speak out against church policies, but then, it could even be someone higher up." She tilted her head and looked at Carter carefully. "We don't know for sure it's murder yet."

"Just a hunch."

The hunch was confirmed the following morning when the first test results came back positive for cyanide. Both in the vomit, in Grigg's system, and in one of the other cookies. Carter and Andreason started contacting the others on their list.

First was Bobby Rasmussen, a sixteen-year-old they pulled out of his high school class. He confessed that he'd talked to the bishop about masturbation. "I was so relieved when he told me not to worry about it," the boy said, making sure no one was in the hallway to hear them. "He just said never to tell any other bishops, that some of them were stuck in the past. It's *never* been a sin, he told me. It's just that some members *think* it is."

Their next contact was Susan Greer, who said the bishop encouraged her to study abroad rather than go on a mission, that he'd prayed and felt that was Heavenly Father's will for her. Steve Munsen said the bishop told him to marry his boyfriend but to do it secretly and pretend they were just roommates. Andy Peterson said the bishop told him it was okay to pay tithing on his "increase" only, not on either his gross or his net, and that it was up to Andy to determine what that increase was.

"What do you think, Andreason?" Carter asked while they sat in the car reviewing their notes. "Seems with some of those radical ideas, he could have a dozen enemies who loathed him."

"Did anyone trace the cookie plate?"

"There was a Deseret Industries sticker on the bottom," Carter replied. "I have Hughes looking at video of anyone buying plates over the past two weeks, but no one's showing up who's a member of Grigg's congregation."

"We better talk to his wife." The woman had asked for some time to herself or Carter would have wanted to start with her first thing in the morning. Women were so delicate, you had to be careful or you'd lose any leads they might offer. He and Andreason drove over to her house now, and Carter tried to let his partner guide this interview as well.

"I feel so guilty," Mrs. Grigg said, wringing her hands. "I shouldn't have left him."

"Left him?" Andreason asked. She stole a glance at Carter.

"On Tuesday, I went to stay with my mother for a couple of days. She's not even an hour away, but that's a different ward, a different stake even, so we don't see each other much. I didn't get back till Thursday afternoon, just before…" She wiped at her eyes. "I left him all alone his last two days. It's unforgiveable."

"Did he ever say any of the members were giving him trouble because of his concerns about doctrine?" Andreason asked.

"Concerns? I don't know what you mean. He was a stalwart member. He supported the Brethren completely." She frowned. "You're not going to try dragging his name through the mud, are you? Our two sons are at BYU. They're both returned missionaries. But they'll be shunned if there's any scandal."

Her eyes became steely. "Some anti-Mormon killed him. There are plenty of those in Salt Lake. Just go to Temple Square and you'll see them. My husband was a martyr."

"What do you think?" Carter asked his partner when they were back in the car.

"She may have done it herself," Andreason replied slowly, "to preserve her husband's reputation. To preserve her own. We might better have people check out DI locations in Spanish Fork where her mother lives and see if there's any video there of her buying a plate." Carter nodded and made a quick call to Hughes.

They only had a few more interviews to do, but Carter's gut wasn't telling him the answer yet. It would, though. He'd solved every murder in the city for the past three years, if you didn't count the ones committed by strangers.

The next interview was with an "inactive" member the bishop visited once a month. "Do you know anyone who might have held a grudge against Mr. Grigg?" Det. Carter asked. He thought he'd better take over the investigation for a while. He'd get to the bottom of this yet.

"Nelson was a teddy bear," Kirk replied. The man was about fifty, not wearing a wedding ring, and sporting trim gray hair.

"Did you talk about the Church much?" Carter pressed. "Did he worry about anyone in particular?"

"We just played chess. Every time he came over. That's all we ever did." He chuckled sadly. "Nelson's favorite piece was the bishop, of course. He always said, 'The bishop's the only one who can move diagonally. Everyone else has to go straight.' Of course, I pointed out that bishops move straight, too, just at a different angle, but he just shrugged and said, 'I like to move between the lines.'" Kirk wrinkled his nose. "Nothing much there to point to a murderer, I'm afraid."

Carter wasn't satisfied with the information coming from the other Mormons and suggested they interview a few coworkers from Grigg's accounting firm. Det. Andreason showed her inexperience again by telling Carter she was sure that would lead nowhere. "I know this has something to do with his church," she said. Carter's jaw tightened, and they headed for Grigg's office. They interviewed four of the man's coworkers and didn't find anything of interest.

At first. But Carter could feel his gut trying to talk to him.

"He was really upset about the gay thing," a woman named Roberta in a crisp black and white dress told them. "He kept saying it simply couldn't be true."

"'It' being the Church or the policy?" asked Andreason. Carter let her speak. "Or do you think he'd just discovered something about himself?"

Roberta laughed. "No, he was all man, that's for sure."

Det. Andreason cocked her head.

"Oh, please don't tell anyone," the woman went on. She covered her mouth for a moment but then lowered her hand and went on. "We all treated Nelson like a bishop here, too, even though half of us aren't even Mormon. We were always going to him with our problems. He told Gene it was okay to look at porn. He told me it was okay to have an affair with Gene. Nelson even…he even let me give him a blow job once. Said his wife hated doing it." She shook her head. "So yes, I think he was straight. He even reciprocated a couple of times." She didn't blush.

Carter and Andreason gave each other a steady look. The motives and list of suspects had just grown larger, not smaller. "That's the way you 'treat a bishop'?" Andreason asked.

Roberta put her hand on the detective's arm. "I only meant we could talk to him about anything. But really, he seemed to feel more and more as if nothing mattered. He used to sing 'Anything Goes' all the time these last few weeks. It's a happy song, but he didn't seem very happy." She squeezed Andreason's hand. "Please don't tell his wife. The only thing he believed was truly a sin was hurting someone. This would hurt her. Please don't say anything."

Yes, thought Carter with a grimace, he was sure the last thing Roberta wanted to do was hurt Mrs. Grigg. Was there anyone more insensitive than a woman? A non-member woman at that. He and Andreason walked back to their car, but before they climbed in, Carter shook his head. "I don't see how we can keep this from blowing up in everyone's face. Somebody killed that bishop, and the reasons aren't going to be pretty."

Det. Andreason didn't say anything, so they sat back in the car. "Where to now?" Carter asked. He thought a second visit to the wife might pay off. She had the biggest motive—revenge, obviously, and the protection of her family's reputation. They would have to interview Mrs. Grigg's mother and see if her daughter had acted oddly during the visit.

"I think it's time we checked Mr. Grigg's debit and credit card transactions," Det. Andreason said calmly.

Carter frowned. "Why? What do you expect to find?"

She shrugged. "Maybe some cookie dough."

"What?"

"Of course, he may have paid in cash, so we'll have to look at video, too, but we'll find him buying it." She looked into Carter's blank face and shook her head.

"Don't you see? He was falling apart, and I think he saw that keeping it from his wife was a losing battle. This was a suicide, Carter. It wasn't Mrs. Grigg trying to protect the family reputation. It was Nelson. Nobody we talked to was angry with him for the radical things he said. They all loved him for it. But he'd lost his faith. Probably some time ago. He must have felt it would be easier for his family if they thought he'd died a believer. And I think he wasn't going to be able to keep it a secret much longer, one way or another."

She sighed. "We'll find that he bought that plate from Deseret Industries, too. And he somehow got hold of the cyanide. And made those cookies while his wife was away and stashed them in his office. Now that we know what we're looking for, it shouldn't be too hard to confirm."

Det. Carter breathed out heavily, his head whirling. What was Captain Jeffries going to say? A case solved in one day! He stole a glance at his partner. "You're right," he said slowly. "I'm sure of it." He chewed his lip.

Andreason sighed again and buckled her seat belt. "Don't worry. It'll be your win. Like always."

Carter shook his head with a smile. What a gal. "Great work, Detective!" She would be his equal one of these days.

Andreason slapped the dashboard. "Let's go."

Next to Murder

"Here, Liam," said Terry. "Right here. No. Here." They set their 150-pound load against the glass doors, just barely catching the body when it began to tip over. Terry steadied the shoulder once, then again. Liam looked at him and shook his head. Terry nodded in return. Next time, they'd have to bring some of that wide, clear packing tape. They could then tape the body's burial clothes to the door with long strips of the adhesive, keeping the body in place.

"Here. Let me put this Book of Mormon in his hands." Terry placed the book of scripture on the body's lap and turned to a random page, positioning both hands to hold the book open.

"Let's get the hell out of here, Terry!"

Terry and Liam stepped back briefly to assess what they'd done. They'd agreed not to take any photos, not to leave any letters, not to make any phone calls. Their actions would have to speak for themselves. They gave each other a peck on the lips and then rushed back to their pick-up, driving off quickly, the trailer carrying their towable backhoe rattling far too loudly behind them. It was almost three in the morning.

The men were too hyped to sleep when they returned to their home in Sugar House. They left the tarps and shovels in the back of the truck, the trailer still hitched to the post. Terry had told Liam right from the start that if the police ever suspected them, they wouldn't try to hide what they were doing. Consequences were part of civil disobedience. There'd be enough DNA and fibers everywhere to convict them. But even the trial would give publicity to the problem they were showcasing.

Liam showered first, then Terry. They put their clothes in the washer and lay on the bed in their fresh garments. Terry took Liam's hand and held it as they lay in the darkened room in silence, waiting for morning. He felt like Leonardo da Vinci or Michelangelo. They were creating a great work of performance art, art that would shake the world every bit as much as the Mona Lisa or the Sistine Chapel.

"Terry. Terry! Wake up! The news is on. Let's see if they say anything."

Terry staggered to his feet and stretched with his eyes closed. After a few sluggish moments, he trudged out to the living room and sat on the sofa next to his husband. The news anchor was halfway through the story about the exhumed body discovered on the front steps of the Mormon chapel. "…appears to be that of Devin Kimball, the young man who committed suicide in Murray three days ago. Authorities have only confirmed that Kimball's grave was tampered with, but they will not confirm if his body was removed from the cemetery. Kimball, as we reported Wednesday, apparently killed himself in response to being called into a disciplinary council by the LDS Church. Neither Church leaders nor…"

Liam grabbed Terry's hand. "We did it," he said. "You were right."

"I don't know," Terry replied. "They still don't seem to have made the full connection."

"Everyone knows the kid killed himself because he was gay."

"They'll just think whoever did this is a creep."

"We *are* creeps. So what? They'll remember that young man every time they open the front doors of the chapel. He won't just be brushed out of their thoughts forever."

They watched the rest of the report. Then the anchor moved on to discuss upcoming traffic delays. What they'd done might be reported again later in the evening news, but by tomorrow, it would be ancient history. Of course, Terry had known from the beginning it was going to take more than one body. Today was Saturday. He and Liam had deliberately chosen the weekend for their first protest. They couldn't jeopardize their careers, after all. Terry was a loan officer at Zions Bank and Liam was produce manager at Carlsons.

"Let's go back to sleep," Terry said. "We'll have a picnic later and then get ready for tonight."

"I love you," Liam told him. He leaned forward, Terry pulling him close so they could kiss. Liam had the worst breath of anyone Terry had ever known. His husband smelled like a rotting corpse himself most of the time. But what could Terry do? He loved the man, so they kissed at every opportunity.

Liam also had a problem with heavy dandruff. He saved the dead skin cells that sloughed off every day to use in the compost for all their gardening, a back yard full of native plants. And the man had what was apparently an incurable case of athlete's foot. The itching may have been what concerned Liam most, but it was the smell that could turn Terry's stomach.

Still, Terry could never get enough of the man. The two had met at a mission reunion four years earlier, bonding over a discussion of black orchids. Terry had been a zone leader in Belize two years after Liam had been an assistant to the president there. They sometimes put on their old nametags when they were feeling adventurous and pretended to be companions helping each other out during "Dual Study." Other times, Terry would be a demanding zone leader to a greenie missionary, and other times Liam would be the sole missionary while Terry played the investigator. They did a lot of deep, thorough investigating.

Liam drove them to Fairmont Park around noon. It was already too warm a summer for some residents to venture outdoors at this time of day, so they were able to find a table quickly. Terry set down his cooler with the chicken salad sandwiches and the plastic containers of chilled applesauce while Liam set his cooler filled with drinks down on the table beside it. "I have a special treat for today," Liam said.

"Funeral potatoes?" Terry asked.

"Don't mock the dead."

"Sorry."

Liam reached into his cooler and brought out two chilled cans of Nestea. He handed one to Terry, who took it with his mouth agape. Liam pulled the tab on his own can and tipped the liquid into his mouth. "Ahhh!" he said.

Terry sat staring at his unopened can. "Are we really going to become complete degenerates now?"

"Terry, if we've become graverobbers, I don't think breaking the Word of Wisdom will be the issue keeping us out of the Celestial Kingdom."

Terry nodded, wondering about all the unintended consequences of calling out the Church on its homophobia. He opened his tea and took a sip. A little tart but still pleasing. But of course, sin always tasted good.

"Someone posted an article on Facebook about how all the suicides in Utah are a result of the high altitude," Terry said, taking a bite of his sandwich.

"Isn't Denver the 'mile-high city'?" asked Liam. "How do the suicide rates compare?"

Terry took another sip of tea. "I'm not sure, but one has to wonder why the suicides seem so much higher among gay people in Utah. Are they taller than straight people?"

"You're taller than I am, Terry." Liam smiled as he chomped on his own sandwich. "I hope you're still taking your Prozac. But I don't expect the altitude here in Salt Lake changes from month to month, yet the suicides keep going up every time the Church makes another hateful statement."

Terry finished his tea and looked at his empty container. "You have any more, sweetie?"

Liam smiled and pulled out another can.

They retired that evening right after watching an episode of *Vicious* on PBS, but even after some exhausting sex, it was hard for Terry to fall asleep. Liam started dozing within minutes, breathing through his mouth, the smell of death wafting toward Terry's face. He didn't think it would ever be possible to like the scent, but the odor was becoming less offensive every day. He wondered if after the resurrection, Liam would still smell the same. Would Terry need to adapt to his husband all over again?

What other changes would there be once they arose from the dead with perfect bodies? Perhaps Terry's anus would be more accepting. Maybe Liam's penis would grow larger. Or, better yet, smaller. But the entire idea of the resurrection left Terry more and more baffled. A really *perfect* body would have *two* penises, one in the regular spot but another on the forehead, so he could suck his partner's second dick at the same time he was getting fucked with the first. Of course, what he'd do with his own extra dick during their lovemaking he didn't know. They probably needed more holes, too.

Perhaps a perfect body would have movable and interchangeable parts. A big dick today. A smaller one tomorrow. Two the day after. Maybe three on Sundays. There would still be Sabbath sex, wouldn't there?

It was difficult to look at paintings LDS artists had created of God the Father and think that was the image of human perfection.

Terry eventually fell asleep, and then at 1:30, the alarm rang. After ensuring their shovels and tarps were still safe in the back of the pick-up, they headed for the next cemetery. Their commitment to gardening was the primary reason for buying the truck three years earlier, but it sure came in handy when one wanted to dig up suicide victims as well.

They'd considered just renting the small backhoe, but that sounded like a sure way to be tracked down quickly, so they'd purchased it in Idaho over a month ago, waiting nervously for the day they'd finally be able to put it to use, dying inside as new reports of other gay youth killing themselves aired regularly on the news. They worked more quickly tonight, pausing briefly only to make sure they hadn't been spotted.

Liam pried open the lid of the casket, and Terry breathed a sigh of relief. Sealed caskets cost more, but the sixteen-year-old kid they were after tonight had shot himself in the head, so the casket had been closed for both the wake and funeral. Closed but not sealed. They pulled the body up out of the grave and dragged it over to the truck.

Terry felt like Victor Frankenstein. Graverobbing to create life, for the thousands of other gay youth who might not take their own lives if the Church could be pressured to stop teaching gay kids to hate themselves.

"Oh, man," said Liam. "I don't think they embalmed this one. Just refrigerated him."

The smell was noticeable, but Terry wondered how Liam could distinguish the smell of death from his own breath. He seemed oblivious most of the time about his continual odor, only worried when he first woke up in the morning, as if his breath were normal any other time of the day.

"Let's stash him in the truck and then load the backhoe on the trailer."

They froze for a moment when they saw headlights pass but then continued. Breaking through cemetery gates would have seemed unimaginable only six months ago, but the number of gay runaways, gay and lesbian kids kicked out of their homes onto the streets, young gay men and women facing excommunication, young transgender folk shunned at work and school, even older LGBT Utahns facing backlash, was increasing all the time.

While society at large grew more understanding, Mormon leaders just cracked down harder and harder. Young people weren't exposed to the world enough to understand there were options. They only understood they were loathed by others as much as by themselves. What good was it to move to San Francisco or Chicago or New York if you were still an abomination to God?

"Did you guys ever break any laws in Belize?" Terry asked, standing in the back of the truck, pulling while Liam pushed.

"You mean like breaking into sports fields to play soccer?"

Terry nodded. "Or baptizing kids without getting their parents' permission," he said. "Or shoplifting food." The mission president had been so stingy with Terry's stipend. And it was all Terry's own money. He'd saved the entire amount himself before he received his call.

"We never felt guilty," Liam said as they covered the boy with the tarp. "Stealing for the Lord was what Nephi did, wasn't it?"

"I've been trying to put my finger on why I don't feel bad now about what we're doing." They worked quickly to secure the miniature backhoe in place.

"What's the penalty if we're caught?"

Terry had never bothered to look it up. "What's the penalty if we do nothing?" he returned. He could have either dead flesh on his hands or blood from the victims he didn't even attempt to save.

Liam gave him a kiss after they climbed back into the front seat and turned on the ignition.

Rotting flesh was better than blood.

They drove to Eric Smoot's ward meetinghouse and quickly deposited the body against the front door. They remembered to bring the tape this time, so positioning the body went more smoothly. Terry placed an open copy of the *Ensign* in the body's lap.

"Let's get out of here," Liam said. They hurried to the truck and back to Sugar House.

How did bank robbers do it, Terry wondered? Bank after bank, the risk of being caught ever greater. Perhaps addiction to money made those guys reckless. But addiction to justice wasn't much safer. He and Liam had to keep going until they made their point. Until their point made a difference.

The sad thing was that they'd never run out of ammunition. Not anytime soon. Terry wondered if it was wrong to use the destroyed bodies of young people as weapons. But even if it were, was it more wrong than Mormons loving their gay family members to death?

Terry was able to fall asleep more quickly this morning, resting his head on Liam's chest, fingering his husband's garment symbols until he fell unconscious. They had set the alarm for 7:00 so they could watch the morning news on KUTV. "There's nothing about the kid," Liam said. "What gives?"

"Maybe no one's shown up at church yet," Terry replied.

They went to their own ward for services later, and no one there seemed aware of what had happened. Bishop Haas pulled Terry aside after Elders Quorum, making his heart skip a beat, but all he said was, "Really, Terry, you need to start attending more Singles dances and find a nice girl to marry. Why do you want to keep living with a roommate like Liam?"

"We served in the same mission. This way we get to keep up the language."

Bishop Haas then cornered Liam. His response was the same as Terry's. The bishop never got the joke.

There was no talk among the ward members about dead bodies during the entire three-hour block.

But finally, on the 5:00 news, it was the lead story. Terry watched, waiting for the reporter to show her interview with one of the apostles.

It never came.

"They're still not saying anything about the suicides being gay," said Terry. "They just keep talking about anti-Mormons and crap like that. Acting like it's a sick prank."

"The members of the wards know, though," Liam reminded him. "They know. The newscasters know, too. They're just pretending so they can downplay it."

"Goddammit." Terry held his hand over his mouth as Liam looked at him in surprise. Then Liam headed for the kitchen.

"Want a beer?" he asked, pulling two from the back of the fridge.

"Alcohol now?" asked Terry. "And so the downward path to the gutter continues."

"I simply think we need something to help us relax. I'm not advocating a fifth of Bourbon. Or two thirds. Or whatever it is."

Terry nodded and opened his Red Rock.

There was talk at work on Monday and Tuesday about the exhumations, but by Wednesday, the city was back to normal. Fortunately, there were no new gay suicides during the week, or at least none reported as such, so on Friday night, Terry pulled up a map of the cemetery where Gerald DeSalvo had been buried three weeks earlier. He was eighteen and had just received his mission call to Nova Scotia when he hung himself in the back yard of his parents' house.

His nine-year-old brother discovered him, a kid old enough to be accountable for cursing his father on camera later when the man said "I would rather my son be dead than lose his chastity" to a reporter. The father denied the boy was gay, but the girlfriend confirmed that Gerald had confessed his feelings toward other young men.

Fortunately, he'd been embalmed, but the procedure was of limited help tonight. A body in the ground that long was still pretty awful to drag to the back of the truck. This time,

Terry and Liam broke into the DeSalvos' ward building and set the corpse up against the bishop's office door. Terry placed a copy of the Bishop's Manual in the body's decaying hands.

They didn't watch the news the following day. They had a picnic in their own back yard around noon, drinking beer with their microwaved hot dogs. Neither of them had much to say. At one point, a terrible odor filled the air. Terry gave Liam a look, but he seemed oblivious. It was a case of SBDAD—Silent But Deadly And Dangerous. Liam's gas smelled worse than the average fart, and he never seemed to notice.

Late in the afternoon, they took a nap in their garments. Terry awoke first and looked down at his husband's still body, his face pressed against the mattress. He leaned over to kiss him on the cheek and took in the smell of death from his breath. He started to get hard. He reached over and gently tried to lower Liam's bottom garments.

"Mmm," he murmured. "Whaaa?"

"Don't move," Terry whispered. "Pretend you're dead, and I'm showing you that our love will endure beyond death." He grabbed some lube from the bedside table.

Liam turned over and sat up. "What?" He wasn't smiling.

They were still spiraling out of control, past the gutter, toward Outer Darkness.

"Let's watch some TV," said Terry. "And make plans for the next body."

They had beer with dinner later and then watched another episode of *Vicious*. They planned how to dig up Chester McConkie's body at yet another cemetery out near Bountiful. Chester had suffered a nervous breakdown after being sexually assaulted by his mission companion in Iceland, being sent home to recuperate.

But it turned out the breakdown occurred because he'd enjoyed what had happened, even the violent aspect. When he finally confessed this part of the event to his stake president, the man set up a court of love to be held the following week. Chester had overdosed on his mother's heart pills the day before the hearing. His note explained that he deserved to be killed, and if his companion hadn't finished the job, he'd have to take care of it himself.

This time, Terry and Liam placed the body on top of the sacrament table. Chester had died a little over a month ago.

The *Trib*, the *DN*, all the local news stations, and now even some cable channels were covering what was going on. The fact that these were all gay suicides was impossible to deny any longer.

"It's working," said Liam. "You're a genius, Terry."

Terry leaned over and kissed Liam, thrusting his tongue deep into his husband's foul-smelling mouth. If only Terry could taste Liam's resurrected breath. If only they each had two glorified penises. Or three.

Tuesday night after work, Terry toasted Liam with a glass of tea. "Let's do a session at the temple tonight," he said.

Liam groaned. "We'll get out so late. I have bananas coming in the morning."

Terry nodded. "But we won't be able to keep our recommends for long. We're going to be found out. No amount of pretending to be straight roommates is going to hold up after that."

Liam rubbed his chin. "I suppose we're lucky no one ever found out we were legally married last year."

"Let's do an endowment session."

They grabbed their suitcases and headed downtown. The Salt Lake temple had to be one of the Church's most beautiful edifices. Really one of the loveliest buildings in the entire country.

Too bad there was no way to get a body past the front desk.

Terry and Liam sat next to each other during the interminable program, helping each other with tying this strap and that. They never took part in the prayer circle, since it was always boy girl boy girl, but tonight, Terry considered it, wondering if he could insist on holding Liam's hand. The feeling passed, and soon they were through the veil and sitting on a luxurious powder blue sofa in the Celestial Room.

"Move along, boys," an elderly woman told them, trying to usher them out to the hall and back toward the dressing area. "Make room for the others."

"Liam…"

"I know, Terry."

"There are consequences for our actions."

Liam nodded.

Terry removed the pocketknife he'd hidden in his white pants. Even now, he wasn't sure what he was going to do. Kill Liam and then himself? Perhaps just himself? Maybe one of the veil workers. Or even one of the younger patrons who'd gone through tonight. He could piss on the veil, force himself to vomit on the altar. He'd be condemned no matter what he did.

What would make the biggest impact?

He stood up, offering his free hand to Liam, the knife in his other. Liam stood as well. Terry pulled Liam close and planted his most fervent kiss ever on the man's lips. There was the sound of a roomful of gasps, a whooshing noise so loud Terry suspected something similar might accompany the creation of a new planet, like the ones he and Liam would make one day.

The sound was followed by shouts of "Hey!" "Stop that!" "What do you think you're doing?" from three elderly temple workers, one of them walking slowly toward them with a cane.

Closing his knife, Terry slipped it back into his pocket and kept kissing. He'd never felt more alive in his entire life. And Liam's breath had never tasted any sweeter.

An Endowed Spy

Jerrod stood at the newsstand and watched the woman walk by. In her mid-thirties, she wore a mottled gray suit coat over a scarlet red skirt, with two-inch heels on narrow-toed red leather shoes. Her shoulder-length hair was almost black, every strand in place. If Jerrod had been a worldly man instead of a faithful Mormon, he might have been attracted to her.

No matter. Silicon had been clear. Jerrod was to approach the woman in a bar, seduce her, and then murder her once inside her apartment.

Not murder. Assassinate. Why did Jerrod keep forgetting the distinction? He'd killed eleven people in the past year since being recruited by the Company after graduating from Brigham Young University with a degree in History. Specifically, Mormon history. Why government agents in the Company felt his studies provided a useful background, Jerrod had never figured out. He'd always expected to teach college Institute classes. His recruiter insisted his selection was due to his missionary service in Austria, but Jerrod had only been assigned to murder one Austrian so far.

Assassinate.

The woman walked quickly up the street, and Jerrod followed briskly but carefully. He'd been observing her the past several evenings, and she had yet to step into a bar at all. But tonight was Friday, and the woman had walked right past her apartment building after getting off the subway. Perhaps tonight she needed a drink.

It had been awkward for Jerrod to take his first drink as part of the job. It had also been awkward the first time he'd had to use sex as a tool. But if killing for his country wasn't a sin, then why should lesser commandments be a problem? Every Sunday, Jerrod went to whichever LDS meetinghouse was nearby and made sure to partake of the sacrament. Then his soul was pure for another week.

The woman pushed open the glass door to a posh bar with a fancy neon sign proclaiming the place a "Delicate Edge." It had certainly been better than the grubby bar called "Rear Entrance" he'd had to frequent for three nights before murdering a dangerous gay hacker last month. He wished he hadn't had to go through with the sex that time before getting down to the killing. But he wasn't a tease.

Jerrod decided to wait on the sidewalk another five minutes to make sure the woman wasn't coming right back out.

Silicon had been gruff with Jerrod when giving him the assignment. "No more of that ritualistic crap," she'd said. "Just strangle her with a scarf."

Jerrod had nodded his acceptance of the order but knew he could never comply. If a person had committed terrible sins, and Jerrod knew no one would be on the elimination list if they hadn't, then they needed more than death. Dying only helped the country. It didn't help the person being murdered.

Assassinated.

If Jerrod had learned anything at all during his four years at Brigham Young, it was that Blood Atonement was essential for people to be forgiven of certain grievous sins. Otherwise, they'd end up in Outer Darkness. Poison wasn't an option. With poison, the person didn't bleed. Strangling wasn't an option, either. Even if there were bruising from the choking, the key feature of Blood Atonement was that the blood be physically shed.

The Church had actively practiced the principle back in the day. Maybe they still did secretly. Gentiles simply didn't understand. It was why Utah continued to have a firing squad for so many years rather than institute hanging or the electric chair. When Jerrod assassinated someone, radiation poisoning was out. So was a blow to the head. Even a gunshot to the head wouldn't work, in Jerrod's opinion. It was essential that the person *be aware* they were bleeding, be aware they were shedding their blood for their sins. Jerrod always made sure to explain it to his victims.

Assignments.

Of course, it was Christ's atonement that did the bulk of the work of forgiveness. It was simply that some particularly bad sins had to be helped along by the blood of the sinner. Brigham Young had been quite clear. And there was no reason Jerrod couldn't serve his country *and* save souls at the same time, was there?

Five minutes had passed, so Jerrod casually entered the building and walked up to the bar without looking about. After ordering a scotch, he leaned against the counter and slowly surveyed his surroundings. The woman was seated at a table three yards away, sitting alone, sipping from a glass filled with a dark liquid. Her eyes were closed, and she leaned her head back, sighing.

Jerrod would disembowel her later. He'd killed all eleven of his assignments either by slitting their throats or disemboweling them. That's the way Mormons were threatened with death in the temple if they ever revealed any secrets, so Jerrod knew that was the way Heavenly Father wanted his non-Mormon children murdered, too.

Silicon had grown increasingly irritated with Jerrod, but he was patient. While killing a woman the ways he had could be disguised as sex crimes, it was difficult to disembowel a high-ranking male military official without it looking suspicious. Jerrod had to prove himself tonight. He had to make things right with the Company.

Could he simply stab this woman in the chest?

Doing such a thing just felt wrong. Jerrod had more than once wondered if he would one day need to atone for his own sins by shedding *his* blood. But that would be like asking every soldier who ever fought in a war to be executed merely for protecting his homeland. Some killings weren't sins. Even Nephi was ordered to kill an unarmed man.

But would there be time for the woman to understand *why* she was bleeding before she lost consciousness? It was essential she understand. Jerrod didn't want to be cruel.

The woman looked toward the bar. Jerrod continued to look in her direction until their eyes made contact. After a brief moment, he turned and looked in another direction. You couldn't seduce someone if you looked too anxious.

Jerrod thought about the endowment session he'd attended the afternoon before. If possible, he enjoyed going to the temple on his assignments in exotic cities. He'd joked to Silicon once he might one day write a story called "Murder with a Recommend." She hadn't looked amused. Some people took themselves too seriously.

Naturally, Jerrod could tell no one about his work. The job made marriage an absolute impossibility. That had worried him at first, since temple marriage was essential for attaining the Celestial Kingdom. But he was only twenty-seven, and by the look on Silicon's face when she gave him this assignment, it might well be his last. He'd disembowel the woman, get fired, and apply with the Church Educational System after all. Tonight would make a dozen murders. Twelve was a righteous number. He could retire without shame after twelve.

Jerrod glanced back toward the woman. She was looking out the window, but a moment later, she turned and looked toward the bar again. Their eyes met and lingered a bit longer this time before Jerrod turned away. He sometimes wondered if the reason he'd been chosen by the Company was solely because of his looks.

He didn't really *want* to retire. He liked his job. He'd never felt so important in his entire life. He was *doing* things.

And guiltless sex wasn't a bad perk. It was as good as having been given the Second Anointing, something only the Brethren received.

Maybe Jerrod would in fact go ahead and stab the woman in the chest. That would satisfy Silicon. Then he could stay with the Company. He could always get married when he was the woman's age. There'd still be plenty of time to raise kids in the gospel.

Taking another sip of his scotch, Jerrod turned casually toward the woman. He stiffened when he realized she was gone. Had she taken off for the bathroom? Had she left the building? Damn!

He just barely caught sight of a red skirt and mottled gray jacket through the front window and jumped up from his stool. He hurried out of the bar and started trying to close the gap between himself and the woman. Half a block behind, he wondered if he'd have to wait for another evening. It wouldn't be the end of the world. The woman might go out again on Saturday night. It wasn't as if these things had to be done immediately.

Still, it would be nice to complete the assignment and wipe the slate clean Sunday morning with a thimbleful of water and a pinched piece of white Wonder bread.

He picked up his pace.

The woman paused to give money to a beggar, and this made Jerrod pause as well. What kind of deadly enemy gave money to beggars? He realized he rarely knew what any of his assignments were guilty of. He was told to take care of them, and that's what he did. It wasn't so very different from obeying his mission president. Or his bishop. Or the prophet.

He'd almost caught up with the woman by the time she started walking again. "That was nice of you," he said, hoping he was close enough she could hear.

The woman turned in confusion as if hearing a buzzing noise, and then her eyes focused on him. "For those to whom much is given, much is required," she said with a smile.

Jerrod tried not to look surprised. "How much did you give him?" he asked. He didn't know why he asked such a question.

"Five dollars. No point giving anything less with the cost of food these days." She shrugged.

"Or the cost of a bottle."

She shrugged again. "Not my place to judge."

Jerrod had become good at small talk but found himself now at a loss for words. Still, he'd made contact. If the woman went back to the bar tomorrow night, he'd have a better chance at connecting then.

"Do you judge people?" the woman asked with a sly smile.

No, Jerrod thought. Someone else does. I'm just the guy who enforces the sentence. "Only if they have particularly sordid sex," he replied. He had to try to be flirtatious.

The woman laughed, a lovely, tinkling sound. "And what qualifies as sordid?" she asked, again smiling as if she had a secret.

"That depends on what we can negotiate." Jerrod smiled, too. The woman looked even more attractive than she had earlier. He felt a stirring in his groin.

"Your suit's quite nice," the woman noted. "Armani?"

Jerrod grinned. It wasn't Armani, but he'd go along.

"And a hundred-dollar tie?"

"A hundred and fifty."

"How often do *you* give to the poor?" she asked, still smiling.

Jerrod paid his tithing. And put aside a little each month for a down payment on a house. There wasn't enough left over for much else. "Would you like to take a walk and give out five-dollar bills tonight?" he asked. He was just trying to catch the woman's interest in some way, but the idea rather intrigued him. Why *didn't* he do things like that?

What could this woman possibly be guilty of?

"Maybe later," she said. "Why don't you come up to my place for a drink first?"

Jerrod smiled. She wasn't into good deeds at all. She probably knew he was watching her all along. Knowing she'd used a homeless man as a tool sent a brief sexual thrill through him.

The woman turned and nodded for him to follow. They were only a few yards from the door to her building, and soon they were in the elevator going up to the fifteenth floor. Her apartment was sleek and modern, clean, with only a single book, closed, on the coffee table. The woman took off her jacket and laid it across the top of a high-backed chair.

"Scotch?" she asked.

Jerrod's eyebrows arched. She'd been watching him at the bar from the beginning. Being *so* attractive had its drawbacks. He preferred the hunt.

"Sure," he said.

"I'm a rum and Coke girl myself," she said. She went to a small bar and prepared the drinks.

She handed him a glass and he took a sip. The woman took a deep sip of hers and leaned her head back and sighed as she'd done in the bar. She had a lovely throat.

Jerrod wanted to slit it.

Still, the woman seemed decent enough. Was it possible he was killing people who didn't deserve to die? He knew it was bad to follow a leader blindly like a mindless sheep, and yet, didn't Jesus always talk about his sheep in a fond, positive way? The scriptures said that obedience was the most important thing, and some prophet, or was it an apostle, had said that being obedient was even more important than being good.

Maybe he should just leave the apartment. Tell Silicon he quit right now. He'd done enough for his country. Someone else could take over for a while. Even God didn't expect a missionary to serve forever.

If he had sex with the woman, without the intent to kill her, would *that* be a sin?

She really did have a lovely throat. She could probably take all of him before he stabbed her in the chest.

Jerrod looked at the woman, sitting on the sofa with her legs crossed demurely, and wanted nothing more in the whole world than to marry her.

How ridiculous.

He put his hand on his suit pocket and felt for his knife.

"You know," the woman said softly, looking at him with a coy expression, "I always like to tell my assignments why I'm killing them."

Jerrod gasped involuntarily, just at the same moment he felt his heart burning as if it were on fire. He put his hand on his chest and staggered to the chair where the woman's coat had been placed so carefully.

"When we have dupes killing U.S. allies, we always figure they'll catch on sooner or later they've been playing for the wrong team. One year is the most we ever give anyone."

Jerrod could hardly hear the last words, the blood drumming in his ears so loudly. It felt as if that man from Rear Entrance was sitting on his chest again.

More than fear, though, Jerrod felt anger.

Why couldn't the woman be decent enough to have sex with him before she killed him? Jerrod was always considerate. He was reasonably well-endowed. It was the least he could do for his victims.

Assignments.

No. Victims.

Jerrod fumbled with his suit jacket, trying desperately to pull out the knife and slice his own throat before he stopped breathing, but his hands wouldn't work. He fell onto the floor and looked up into the woman's beautiful face.

So incredibly rude not to disembowel him. How could she be so cold?

"This isn't even my apartment," she said, still sitting calmly.

Jerrod thought of missionary devotionals, and Seminary classes, and BYU student wards, and the pretty young girls he'd passed up for his job. He thought about Celestial rooms and General Conference and Fast and Testimony offerings.

He was a good man.

His last thought was whether there'd be Institute classes to teach in hell.

The Whopper

I was sitting in a pew, four rows from the front of the chapel, with my wife Megan and our three-year-old son Samuel, singing along with the Sacrament hymn, when the aroma hit me.

Cheerios.

Not only did Samuel have a small sandwich bag full of them to keep him happy during the long meeting, but kids in the families on either side of us did as well.

Now I have to say, I've never been all that fond of Cheerios. Growing up, I ate Cap'n Crunch and Fruity Pebbles. Cheerios was far too bland for my satisfaction. Unfortunately, those self-indulgent tastes had stayed with me in adult life. Even so, the smell made me hungry. Megan had put her foot down just two weeks ago, demanding I lose the extra ten pounds I was carrying. "If you're ten pounds overweight at the age of twenty-eight, it's only going to get worse. We have to nip this in the bud."

She prepared salads for dinner every night now, and broiled fish, and baked, skinless chicken. It was all certainly tasty enough, but sometimes, I just wanted to sink my teeth into a fat, juicy burger.

The Snickers I'd treated myself to last Wednesday at work was a distant memory.

I stole a glance at my watch. It was only 10:20. Our three-hour block had barely started, and it was hours yet before we'd be home and able to eat lunch. Why I was so hungry only two hours after breakfast I didn't know. Unless it was because I never found oatmeal all that satisfying, either. It wasn't even Fast Sunday, and I was desperate for a snack. There was a granola bar stashed in the glove compartment of the car. Was there any way to sneak out to the parking lot unseen?

Samuel sneezed, and I patted his head. He was coming down with a cold and had been fussy all day.

When the sacrament tray came by a few minutes later, I took an extra bite of bread. The additional five calories did nothing for me. As the youth speaker stumbled over his words, and the oldest violin player in existence screeched out a special musical number later, I dreamed about Burger King.

I wanted a Whopper.

The question was—how was I going to get one?

There was no way I could wait until services were over and make a casual suggestion on the way home. Even if fast food itself wasn't taboo in our household, there was still the sin of doing business on the Sabbath. No, this was going to take some planning.

Sunday School was next, and Samuel was shipped off to the Nursery, whining a little because he wasn't feeling well. As I listened to our teacher in Gospel Doctrine explain his take on the miracle of the fishes, I thought about Whoppers.

"So we see that Heavenly Father will always provide," the teacher went on. "We don't need to worry about dwindling resources and having too many children. There will always be enough food for everyone in God's kingdom."

There wasn't enough food in my own refrigerator, I thought. I had to have that burger.

During the closing prayer, throwing out an extra degree of sincerity heavenward, I was given a revelation: take Samuel for a ride. I had contemplated skipping out of Priesthood class for the last meeting of our block while Megan went to Relief Society for that final hour, but it was simply too risky. What if someone saw me leave and made some reference to Megan? What if I left, had my burger, but when I returned, the congregants from the succeeding block who shared our building had started to arrive, and someone had taken our parking space? It would be clear then I'd taken off, with or without anyone making a comment.

No, it was just too risky. But if I went to the Nursery to check on Samuel, and decided he needed a ride to make him feel better…well, that might work.

"Have fun in Relief Society," I said as everyone in class started to stand up. "I'll go check on Samuel." I gave Megan a kiss.

"Oh, Ned, he'll be fine. Don't baby him."

"Only want to make sure. I'll just peek in."

Megan rolled her eyes and headed for her next class, and I tried to keep myself from running down the hallway. I went into the class for the three-year-olds, and in fact Samuel did seem kind of fussy. The young woman tending him seemed all too happy to relinquish him to my care.

But as we walked to the car, I began to see flaws in my plan. We couldn't simply drive to Burger King. Samuel was sure to say something to his mom about it. "Hey, buddy," I said, strapping him into his seat, "how about we go get you a little medicine to make you feel better?"

"Okay, Daddy." He had that special vocal tone that indicated he was almost ready for a nap.

Grinning, I pulled out of the parking lot and headed for the nearest drugstore. It was sixty degrees outside, so I risked leaving Samuel in his car seat while I ran into the store. I wanted him to doze, and getting him in and out of the car might rouse him too much. I rushed down the cold and flu aisle and grabbed a bottle of Nyquil. The nighttime kind. The one with alcohol.

I paid with cash so there'd be no danger of a transaction showing up on our joint debit card with today's date and ran back to the car before someone reported me to the authorities for child endangerment. Samuel was almost asleep, but I managed to force a whole capful of Nyquil down his throat.

My kid was going to grow up an alcoholic. All because I wanted a Whopper.

I stole a glance at my watch again and realized I needed to hurry. Burger King was only three blocks away. I ran through a yellow light to get there. Two cars were ahead of me in the drive-thru. Hmm. Maybe the counter would be faster. But I couldn't risk leaving Samuel alone again. I looked over my shoulder and saw his head drooping forward over his chest. I chose the drive-thru, tapping impatiently on my steering wheel as the woman in front of me dawdled.

I suddenly noticed I was the only person in the area wearing church clothes. I felt another pang of guilt, and when it was finally my turn to order, I almost whispered into the microphone.

"A Whopper," I murmured softly.

"Will that complete your order?" The girl spoke so loudly.

"Yes, thank you," I hissed. I looked over my shoulder again, but Samuel was oblivious.

She blared out the price, and I pulled up to wait for my turn at the window.

And finally, gratefully, miraculously, three minutes later I had the most wonderful burger in the world in my hands. I inhaled deeply, almost dizzy, and pulled forward. I parked in the restaurant parking lot, glanced over my shoulder to make sure Samuel was still asleep, and opened the wrapper. I closed my eyes for a moment and offered thanks to Heavenly Father for the meal, feeling immediate guilt as I did so.

But I was going to eat the damn thing, even if it damned me.

The grilled meat was so wonderfully tasty. The tomato, the pickles, the onions, the ketchup, the mustard—it was all just too lovely. I was in heaven.

Though I was probably going to hell for what I was doing. What was wrong with me? The Church was all about self-control. How was I ever going to make it to the Celestial Kingdom if I couldn't wait till Monday during lunch at work to sneak in my Whopper?

I took another huge mouthful just as Samuel twisted behind me in his car seat and whined. I almost choked, but Samuel didn't open his eyes.

Careful not to let any condiments drip on my white shirt, I finished the last bite, my eyes rolling back in my head like a shark's when it attacks. I put the wrapper back in the bag, jumped out of the car to throw the evidence away, and then opened the trunk to hide the Nyquil bottle. I'd have to take it to work with me tomorrow and leave it at the office. I hoped Samuel was too drugged and too sleepy and too young to form a strong memory of having taken the medicine. Perhaps he wouldn't say anything to Megan about it.

I drove quickly back to church, and with relief found that our original parking space was still available. So should I tell my wife I'd attended Priesthood, after all, or should I tell her I took Samuel for a ride? She hated when I missed Priesthood, especially when I used Samuel as an excuse. I'd never rise to become a High Priest if I didn't show my zeal as an elder first.

The guilt I now felt for jeopardizing my rise in the hierarchy left a bad taste.

I would tell Megan I went to Priesthood meeting, I decided. I popped an Altoid in my mouth to cover the odor of the Whopper and then carefully extracted Samuel from his car seat. He murmured but remained asleep in my arms. I walked carefully back to the foyer and arrived just at 12:58.

I looked quickly in the direction of the Relief Society room. They hadn't let out yet. I breathed a sigh of relief.

A moment later, I saw Megan walking to the foyer with several of the other sisters. "Oh, you picked up Samuel already?" she asked.

"Priesthood let out early."

"Well, that was very sweet of you. Thanks."

"No problem."

"What did you guys talk about today?" she asked.

"Bearing false witness," I blurted. It was the first thing that came to mind.

"Interesting. We talked about the role of women, how our spirits are so special we don't need the priesthood the way you men do."

"Yes?" It was great she was still absorbed by her class. We walked outside and down the sidewalk toward the car.

I wished I'd had a double cheeseburger chaser.

"The teacher explained that the priesthood is just a crutch for men because they're weaker." She patted Samuel's hair as we reached the car and started inserting him back into his car seat. He whimpered again but remained asleep.

I wondered if I could sneak in another Whopper this week. Maybe on Wednesday. I always needed a treat on Wednesday to help me through the rest of the week.

I wished I were already a High Priest and not just an elder. I needed sturdier crutches.

After Megan and I strapped our seatbelts on as well, I started to back up. I looked over at the meetinghouse and wondered if I was going to be able to partake of the sacrament next Sunday after all my sins today. I really *had* to, of course, or Megan would start to wonder. So that would be adding yet another sin, partaking unworthily of the sacrament.

It was just one sin on top of another.

Maybe I should make an appointment to talk with the bishop. Or maybe I could bear my testimony next Fast and Testimony. I didn't really *know* the Book of Mormon was true, but we were told to bear our testimony *until* we knew. I could encourage other people to believe and be better people, even if I was destined for the Telestial Kingdom myself.

"What would you like for lunch, dear?" Megan asked as we pulled out into the street. "Sunday meals are special, you know."

"Those salads you make are always yummy," I replied, glancing over at and smiling.

"Good for you! You are so easy to please," she said, laughing. "I wish every Mormon wife could have a husband like you."

I stared down the road ahead of me, my hands gripped tightly on the steering wheel. I felt a bead of sweat on my forehead and flipped open the vent. I pushed the button for the CD player, and soon the Mormon Tabernacle Choir began drifting softly into the car.

Dear Abish

As a Mormon advice columnist, I suppose it was only natural I had a confession of my own to make. My complaint was that I had to write under a pen name, and the world would never know how wise and profound I really was.

As an attorney in the Church Office Building, I was still hoping to move up the ladder. But the fact was that Church employees rarely became General Authorities. It was kind of like the maid expecting to become lady of the house at some point. It wasn't happening in *that* house.

So I started gathering the most interesting letters from my column at the *Deseret News*. And, of course, my most brilliant responses. I hoped to publish a collection called *Our Dear Abish Knows*, but not with Deseret Book. I wanted national publication. I really thought I could claw my way up onto the *New York Times* bestseller list. Then maybe the Church would finally notice me.

Though I'd been writing for a few years, no one in the COB knew I was moonlighting. Not even my wife Caroline knew. She sometimes knocked on my office door at home and asked, "Why are you giggling in there?"

"Just reading some memes on Facebook," was my usual reply.

But then she always asked if she could see, too. Awkward. Since Caroline was a devoted fan of Abish, I made up my own letter one day to address the issue.

Dear Abish,

My husband is a stalwart priesthood holder, but lately I've begun to grow suspicious he has become addicted to the New Drug. I hear him giggling in his home office while working on the computer, and he never lets me see what he is looking at. What can I do to save my marriage?

Signed, Concerned Homemaker

Dear Housewife,

Every man needs downtime for himself. It doesn't mean he is sinning. As a goddess in heaven, there will be lots of times you won't be able to monitor your husband's every move. You may as well get used to it now. But if you ARE interested in improving your marriage sexually, ask him what new things he wants to try, and be willing to do them. Again, in heaven, you'll need to be creative to keep your marriage interesting for all eternity. Earth life is the time to prepare for the world to come.

To be honest, a great many of the letters I posted were related in some way to something personal going on in my life. Any time there was a disagreement with my in-laws, or even my own parents, for that matter, Abish always rushed in for the rescue.

Dear Abish,

My son-in-law always wants to spend Christmas with his own parents. We get Christmas Eve every year, but HIS parents get the real Christmas. Our daughter goes along with her husband because he's head of the household, but I'M the head of MY household, and my wife says I shouldn't put up with this, that I should insist we share the holidays equally. I don't want to make my wife unhappy, but I don't want to make my daughter unhappy, either. What should I do?

Signed, Second-Class Head

Dear Second Head,

Your signature says it all. It proves you really are a righteous priesthood holder receiving revelation for your family. You ARE in second position. That is always the case when a new generation comes along. You've had your turn at the top. Now it is your son-in-law's turn. The best thing you can do is be gracious about it.

My daughter Betsy turned seventeen recently and wasn't a big follower of the news, but she did make time every day to read my column. I nipped two or three problems in the bud over the past year with that advantage. None of our other kids read me, unfortunately, so when we had a problem with one of them, I had to address the letter and response to my wife so she could act as "interpreter" for the family.

Dear Abish,

Our teenage son says he hates Seminary and insists if we continue to force him to go, he won't serve a mission. But if he starts rebelling now, he'll still never go on a mission. What can I do to help him see the light?

Signed, Mother of Alma the Younger

Dear Mother of a Future Prophet,

See what I did there? You can't think of your son as an apostate. You must think of him as a future GA. It's called "labeling." Give him ten dollars for each week of Seminary he completes. Give him an additional $250 for each year he completes. But don't stop there. Give the boy a full $100 for each Church book he reads on his own, IF he can verbally give you a report on the book's contents and answer some basic questions that prove he didn't just get a summary off the Internet. I know it feels odd to give your son monetary rewards for following commandments, but that is in essence what Heavenly Father does as well. We all know that the most righteous among us are those who receive approval from the Lord in ALL manners. Have you ever seen a man on welfare called as an apostle? You'll be teaching your son a valuable lesson, and you'll end up with the son you want, knowledgeable in the ways of the Lord.

My column gave me an opportunity almost weekly to guide my family through a life full of temptation. I commented on chastity of dress, on the evils of smoking, on not wasting time with computer games. I commented on divvying up household chores, on the importance of family prayer, on dedicating time to homework.

Seeing results within my own walls would have been gratifying on its own, even if I didn't enjoy such a large following. I could be in the grocery store and overhear two women talking about my latest column. I could be walking through the chapel and hear the same thing. Once, I even heard my boss at the COB commenting to a fellow attorney about something I'd written. It was quite flattering. I was really good!

The only problem was I couldn't tell anyone who I was. It was infuriating.

I helped hundreds of readers cope with cancer, with abusive husbands, with cheating wives, with kids on drugs, with grandfathers addicted to pornography, with siblings who left the Church. Because I was a Mormon columnist, I always got the chance to promote the Church while simultaneously helping the helpless. In some ways, it was a more satisfying job than simply monitoring the Intellectual Property of the Church.

Once, I was reprimanded by my editor for suggesting a wife needed to be open to the idea of oral sex. But I pointed out several Church leaders who'd hinted as much. Still, I was forbidden to be that specific and had to revise my column. Another time I had to choose a different letter entirely when I responded comfortingly to a mother who'd just discovered her daughter was lesbian. I'd suggested her condition might come in handy when she had two hundred sister wives in the Celestial Kingdom. But that wouldn't do.

So I picked a letter from a woman irritated that the bishop of her ward always allocated the money raised by the Young Women to the Young Men's activities instead. I informed her that Celestial women weren't bean counters.

I had to say, though, that writing this column for the past three years ended up being as eye-opening for me as for my readers. I heard of Machiavellian moves by stake presidents, Orwellian actions by Relief Society presidents, horror stories from Visiting Teachers. And every single day, I received letters from members who just weren't sure they could keep believing anymore. I assured them only the elect were tested so severely, that there must needs be opposition in all things. But people kept asking the same damn questions week after week. I jumped at every opportunity to address something different.

Dear Abish,

I work in the Church Office Building and interact with some of the General Authorities daily. As I hear them snipe at underlings and see their puffed-up arrogance, my testimony is shaken harder and harder each day. It's not all of them, of course, but there are a couple who make me wonder what Heavenly Father was thinking. What can I do?

Signed, Sleepless in Salt Lake

Dear Sleepyhead,

What can you do? You can get another job. It is probably people like you that make life so challenging and irritating for Church leaders in the first place. They're only human, after all. Get that cat calendar off your desk, repent of speaking ill of the Lord's anointed, and make an extra donation to the Temple Fund.

The day that letter was published, my boss gave me an odd look and removed the cat calendar from his desk. For a while, I was happy again that no one knew who Abish was.

But it was the letter I received a few days later that made me want to publish a complete book, that made me want to come out as Abish. It was the letter that would get me somewhere on that *New York Times* bestseller list. I was going to *be* somebody.

Dear Abish,

I've spent my entire life serving the Lord and have risen quite high in His Church. I can't be too specific, but I'm one of the top six in the Quorum in seniority, and there's no one here I can talk to. Instead of discussing the mysteries of God, they spend all day behind closed doors kvetching about their boring wives. What do you do when you know first-hand you've been telling lies all your life?

P.S. Please edit to hide my identity.

Signed, The Fourth Nephite

To be clear, before going to publication this morning, I changed the one line to "I'm in the Quorum of the Seventy" just to throw sniffers off the track. I wasn't a bastard, after all.

Dear Nephite,

I can only tell you what you have told me. Doubt your doubts and buck up. If you feel so strongly about it, announce you have health problems and get the Church to give you emeritus status. Your followers deserve a leader who leads instead of whines.

I was the Judge Judy of the advice columnist world! My wife commented on my giggling these days even when I wasn't at my computer but just sitting at the table eating.

The thing about that letter was…I fully planned to use the original wording when I published my book. The news would rock the world. At least the Mormon world. And I would make lots of money. And maybe *then* I would finally become lady of the house. I sent off query letters to four literary agents and kept my fingers crossed. I knew this part of the process could take quite some time. So after work today, I went to my office at home and read the latest letters that came my way.

Dear Abish,

My husband is becoming more stuck on himself every day. I thought up a plan to put him in his place, and I worked it out with one of his superiors to trap him into making a fool of himself publicly, to knock him down a peg. I'm afraid when he finds out, he's going to be upset. Should I care?

Signed, A Neil Diamond Song

Boy, I thought, these letters were getting weirder all the time. I tapped my chin for a few moments, rubbed my crotch for another moment, which always helped me focus more completely, and tried to think of a fun answer that would bring me more readers.

The Number of the AC

Bishop Slater was tired. He'd been bishop of the New Orleans Ward for three years now, a tough job even in the best of times, but these past few weeks, more and more of his congregation were scheduling appointments to see him. First, it had been Jimmy Caldwell, the Elders Quorum president, to confess he'd started smoking pot. Then it had been Sarah Castigliano, the Beehive instructor, to confess she'd allowed her husband to film her masturbating and put the video online. And then Henry Adamson, the Boy Scout Cubmaster, and Kathy Jenkins, the ward organist, came in to confess they'd started an affair. And after that, Brother Arceneaux, the first counselor in the bishopric, and Randy Orgeron, the Seminary teacher, ran off downriver to Venice to share a fishing shack together on the bayou, leaving their families behind.

What the hell was going on?

Bishop Slater looked at his computer screen in his office at the back of the meetinghouse on St. Charles Avenue. Ellen Ackerman was the next scheduled appointment. He dreaded what she might say. Almost seventy-nine, surely she didn't have any horrific sins to confess. Perhaps she'd been late returning a library book?

He looked at his watch. Almost 8:30. Betty would be upset if he came home late yet another night. As the youngest bishop to preside over this ward in half a century, Bishop Slater knew he was on his way to greatness in the Church. That wasn't easy for those not living in the "Morridor" of the Intermountain West.

But as much as he wanted to be an Apostle one day, or at the very least a Seventy, he didn't want to sacrifice his family to do so. He wasn't entirely satisfied with marriage, but that wasn't Betty's fault. He toggled to his personal email and started composing a quick love note. "A thousand kisses if you save a slice of roast beef for me," he typed.

He was just about to hit Send when he noticed the far right of his screen, where Yahoo ran ads even while he was in his own account. A chunky but pretty young woman in her late twenties flashed across the screen in a variety of poses wearing a wide selection of dresses, selling stylish garments for plus-sized women.

Gwynnie Bee, he read with a frown.

Why was Yahoo sending him advertisements about women's dresses? Just yesterday, there'd been an ad for jewelry, and the day before that, for Victoria's Secret. An accountant during the day at a large firm headquartered in One Shell Square, Bishop Slater had some vague notion that computers tracked every site one visited and then targeted the owner of the computer with ads for products the owner was likely to be interested in, based on their browsing history.

But as a devout Mormon, he had no desire to buy bright purple bras for his wife. And what in the world made the computer think he was going to select any dress for his wife at all rather than let her pick out her own, however stylish his choice might be? Sure, wives were subject to their husbands, and Betty always acquiesced appropriately, but it wasn't as if he didn't allow his wife *some* basic freedoms. There was always the Golden Rule to remember.

Bishop Slater sent his email and then stood up to let Ellen into his office. He didn't want to keep the woman waiting. Old people went to bed early. "Good evening, Sister Ackerman," he said kindly. "Come sit down and tell me what's on your mind."

She waited for him to close the door and return to his seat before she began to speak. "Bishop Slater," she said so softly he had to lean forward, "it's Albert." She buried her face in her hands.

Sister Ackerman's husband was too frail to attend services these days. Perhaps he'd taken a turn for the worse. Bishop Slater felt guilty for hoping the man was dying rather than sinning like everyone else lately. "What is it?" the bishop asked, trying to dredge up some concern. He was almost out. "Your Home Teachers haven't said anything."

"Oh, no, we would never have told the Home Teachers about this," she said, aghast, "or the Visiting Teachers."

"What is it, dear?" Bishop Slater asked gently. "Do you want to tell me what the trouble is?"

"Oh, Bishop, it's just too awful."

Why the Church didn't routinely call dentists to be bishops, Bishop Slater didn't know. Every confession was like pulling teeth, even when the members volunteered to come in of their own accord. And it sounded like sin again this time, after all, the bishop mused. Gosh darn it.

After another couple of minutes of coaxing, Sister Ackerman finally explained the situation. "We keep getting these emails from President Barkley," she said. She was obviously referring to the stake president. "With all these articles that prove the Book of Mormon isn't true." She shook her head. "Why would he send those to us? We thought he was trying to do outreach, send us little spiritual lessons, since Albert can't come to church anymore, but now…" She sniffed. "…Albert wants to take his name off the rolls of the Church."

"What?" Bishop Slater was dumbfounded.

"He's lived eighty-two years as a stalwart Mormon, a defender of the Book of Mormon at all costs, and now, just before he's about to die, he's falling into apostasy. I don't know what I'm going to do." She wiped her eyes.

Bishop Slater thought quickly. "But *you* don't want to leave the Church, do you, Sister Ackerman?"

She shook her head. "I never read any of the articles. That kind of stuff bores me to tears." She sniffed again.

Bishop Slater nodded. "I'll come out to visit in a couple of days." He looked at his calendar. "Will Saturday around 2:00 be okay?" Sister Ackerman frowned and looked worried, so the bishop continued. "The Saints don't start playing till 4:00."

Sister Ackerman smiled. About to go to hell, the bishop thought, and worried about the damn Saints. He'd never really fit in here in New Orleans. But he wouldn't have to, once he was finally called as a General Authority and could go out west. Once he had a sign that Heavenly Father approved of him despite everything.

The old woman asked for a blessing and Bishop Slater reluctantly gave her one. He always hated giving blessings, feeling like a fraud because of his own weaknesses, but he said some comforting words and then led her to the door. He couldn't help but notice how soft her hair was. He almost asked what kind of conditioner she used but instead quickly ushered her out of the office and returned to his desk. He looked at his computer to check the schedule. Surely, she was the last appointment of the evening.

But no, a late emergency had come up, and Brother Bingham must be waiting out in the hall. Bishop Slater put his hand to his head. He was going to be forced to ask to be released, even if that hurt his chances to keep rising up the hierarchy. All this drama was killing him. He'd simply need some other sign of heavenly approval. He toggled to his private email to see if Betty had emailed back. She had.

"Darling, you are always worth waiting for."

He smiled and was just about to toggle back to his work screen when he noticed an ad for the reality show *I Am Cait*. Bruce, or rather, Cait, was amazingly pretty for a woman her age, Bishop Slater thought. Then he frowned.

What in the *world* had he ever clicked on to make the computer think he'd be interested in such a show?

He stood and let Brother Bingham in. He taught the young men in the Teachers Quorum. "What can I do for you this evening?" the bishop asked, forcing a bright smile.

Brother Bingham sat down, looking devastated. The bishop wondered if the man's wife had cheated on him. Or if he'd cheated on his wife. "Why, Bishop?" he asked, about to cry. "Why did you do it?"

Bishop Slater was bewildered. What could the man possibly be talking about? The bishop certainly had his temptations, his forbidden dreams, but he was as worthy of his temple recommend as anyone in the stake. "Excuse me?"

"Bishop, why did you send me that link?" Brother Bingham demanded.

The bishop shook his head. "I...I'm afraid I'm not following."

"That link to the CES letter," Brother Bingham continued.

Bishop Slater's heart sank. If someone had sent his congregant a link to that diabolical document, they'd done a terrible thing indeed. While he'd never read the infamous letter asking difficult questions of a Church Educational System employee, Church leaders had certainly warned all the local authorities about it and other anti-Mormon rubbish to be found on the internet. "I did not send any such thing," the bishop protested.

Brother Bingham looked at him, his face a mixture of despair and condemnation. "I know you did it," he said. "It came from your email. I trusted you. And I read it. And now…"

"What happened?" the bishop asked.

"My wife and I want you to take our names off the rolls of the Church."

Bishop Slater's head was reeling. Three apostasies in one evening. *What* was happening? With that plus the several Church courts he'd had to convene over sexual sin in the past couple of weeks, the ward was quickly imploding. Soon there'd be no one left but the children in Primary.

"We'll get you some counseling," the bishop began. "We'll pray together, and…"

Brother Bingham stood to leave. "I've told you what to do. You won't be seeing us again." He opened the door and walked out.

Oh, my heck, thought Bishop Slater. He looked about the office desperately, hoping for inspiration. His eyes locked on the framed portrait of the First Presidency on the wall. The bishop grabbed the phone and dialed President Barkley. The stake president would know what to do.

"Please," said a tired voice on the other end of the line, "please don't tell me *you're* leaving the Church like everyone else."

"President Barkley, are you having trouble, too? Half my ward has gone insane."

"Bishop Slater, I've been on my knees for days. Missionaries are coming home from their missions. Relief

Society presidents are having affairs with High Priest group leaders. *Deacons* are asking to be excommunicated." There was a pause, but the bishop didn't know what to say to fill it and let the pause drag out. "I've put in a call to Salt Lake, but I don't know what they can possibly tell me."

"President, call me the instant you hear anything. Maybe it's a sign of the End of the World. The Prophet will know *something*."

He hung up, clicked out of his Church account, and looked at his personal email one last time. Should he write his old mission president and ask for advice? His old bishop from his home ward in Idaho? Maybe the old stake patriarch who'd given him his blessing fifteen years ago. There must be someone with spiritual reserves who could help.

Bishop Slater typed a short email to Betty. "I'm on my way. Can't wait to kiss the love of my life." He had to make sure *his* family stayed strong in the midst of this whirlpool of sin. He hit Send, and just as he was about to log out of his email account, another ad caught his eye. A padded bra that let small-breasted women look full-figured without having to undergo surgery.

The computers were going crazy, too.

Bishop Slater drove home, going slightly over the speed limit, a sin he rarely permitted himself to commit, but he simply had to see Betty now. Hold her, kiss her. Even though it was Thursday night and he was already exhausted, they'd have to make love. He needed help. And Betty was the only one who could give it.

Betty was in a coy mood when Bishop Slater walked through the door. The two girls, aged three and five, were in their bedrooms asleep. Bishop Slater wolfed down some roast beef, chugged some milk, and got ready for bed. He'd just brushed his teeth when the phone rang.

"Don't answer it," Betty called out from the bed, the sheet pulled protectively to her chin. Bishop Slater hoped she didn't plan on using it as a shield tonight.

He smiled a reprimand and picked up the receiver. It was President Barkley. "Bishop Slater," he said breathlessly. "Salt Lake called." He paused again, but only for a second. "The techs at the Church Office Building have discovered what's going on." He paused yet again. It was infuriating.

"Well?"

"It's a computer program. Well, even worse than that. The Church thinks it's some kind of artificial intelligence. This AI is the Anti-Christ. It's finding out everyone's vulnerabilities and trying to destroy the testimony of every single member of the Church. It's only affecting Mormons. No one else even seems to realize this is happening."

They were both quiet a long moment. Bishop Slater didn't know what to say. But those infernal ads were beginning to make sense now.

"Thank you, President," the bishop finally said. "Call me in the morning when you know more. I'm sure the First Presidency will have a plan of defense soon, if not a plan of attack." He hung up the phone.

Then he turned to look at Betty, smiling and bewitching, as if she hadn't a care in the world. Thank goodness she didn't like computers, other than email. She didn't even do Facebook. His family was safe. The girls were too young. They'd make it through all this.

If he could get those ads out of his mind.

He suddenly wondered what kind of ads his wife was seeing on *her* email account. He looked at her again, his brows furrowed, but she was smiling back pleasantly. Then he smiled, too. Perhaps Betty had no vices to manipulate. She was all sweetness all the time. That was why he'd married her.

The bishop stripped to his garments, as he usually did at bedtime, fingering the embroidered symbols he'd learned about in the temple. He rubbed the one over his right nipple for several seconds as he stood looking at the bedside table where he kept his lubricant. But when he started to pull the covers back, Betty shook her head.

"No, sir," she said. "Everything off. Just like me." She threw the sheet back and revealed she was lying in bed completely naked, something they hadn't done even on their honeymoon eight years before. Bishop Slater didn't know what to think now. She *had* seen some kind of ad, he realized. She—

Then he saw she wasn't completely naked, after all. She was wearing…oh, my heck…some kind of device, a strap-on rubber penis.

"Betty," he breathed.

"It came in the mail," she said, "with your note." She giggled. "From some place named Leather Life in the French Quarter." She shook her head. "Let's hope no one looks at your credit card statement!" She wagged her finger at him playfully and then flicked that finger against the penis, making it wave back and forth.

"Betty…"

"I can't believe you've wanted what I've wanted all this time." She smiled and patted the mattress next to her. "We're going to enjoy eternity together," she said.

That Artificial Intelligence might have had his number, thought Bishop Slater, but it didn't know everything. That he could never be persuaded away from the gospel. That the Beast was instead answering his deepest, most heartfelt prayers. He and Betty had a temple marriage. And they were going to stay true to the Lord forever. Now it might actually be possible.

Betty winked at Bishop Slater, and he tore off his garments and jumped onto the bed. He got up on all fours with a big, wide smile, waiting happily for Betty to come in from behind.

A Day at the Temple

"Hey, Ben, look," I said, pointing.

"What?"

"It's the temple."

"Here?"

"They're all over now."

"Well, bully for the Church."

"Ben," I said with a grin, "let's go in."

"Are you crazy, Royd?"

"Just in the lobby," I insisted. "We're wearing white. It'll be okay."

"I don't think it's a good idea."

"For old time's sake."

Ben shrugged, and we headed for the front doors of the massive, white structure. Once inside, we saw a dozen or so people milling about, men, women, and even some children, everyone headed somewhere. We avoided the reception desk and just walked about slowly, trying to get a feel for the place.

As ex-Mormons, it had been years since either Ben or I had gone inside a temple. I'd lived in Miami, where at the time, the nearest temple was in Atlanta, so other than during my brief stint at the Missionary Training Center, when my companion and I had gone every week to the Provo temple, and a couple of times after getting home from Oklahoma, I hadn't been at all. Only about ten or eleven times total.

Of course, the last two of those times were on stake temple trips, where we spent two full days each time, doing four or five endowment sessions a day. Those days were interminably long. All I'd wanted to do was sleep during the Garden of Eden. I'd felt trapped, which was the way I'd eventually felt at church as well, until I finally fled.

My family cut me off, and I thought that was the last I'd ever have to deal with Mormons, until I met Ben. He was ex-Mormon, too, though his family sometimes still spoke to him, about once a year. He didn't miss the Church, either.

If I didn't miss it, why had I come inside the temple during our vacation to this city?

"Over there," I whispered, pointing. It was the sewing room, where old women helped fit garments on first-time temple-goers. We wandered over and watched as they added elastic here and tucked in fabric there.

I remembered my garments. The Church was just experimenting with two-piece garments during the time I first went through the temple. I wanted the "real thing," though, and bought the one-piece. To my surprise, I loved them. They felt so smooth and silky, and there was no undershirt to come unstuffed from my underwear. It was comfortable.

I continued to wear my garments even after I came out. I remembered one of my early dates with a guy I'd met at PFLAG. We went back to his apartment, and I was lying on the sofa with Bryan on top of me. We were kissing, and he finally reached down to unbuckle my belt and unzip my pants.

"You're in for a surprise," I said, wondering how he'd react to the garments.

Bryan had pulled back, shocked and afraid. He wouldn't go any further. Maybe he expected me to have two dicks. All I knew was that if garments were going to prevent me from having sex, I wasn't going to wear them anymore. The next day, I went out and bought "Gentile" underwear and threw my garments away.

All except one pair I kept as a keepsake.

When I met Ben seven years later, we didn't have sex on our first date, but I did learn he was ex-LDS. I didn't let on that first evening I was a former Mormon, too, but I deliberately wore the garments on our next date, determined to have a little fun with him. When we undressed, Ben freaked out. I told him I was an undercover Mormon trying to find former members. He almost ran out of the room until I told him I was joking. We now only wore the garments on our anniversary, when we had especially perverted sex. We'd just celebrated twelve years together.

"Can I help you boys?" asked one of the old women, with a needle in her hand. "Come here and let me measure you."

We nodded politely and moved on.

"We should really leave now," Ben whispered.

"Okay," I agreed. "This way."

We walked down a hallway which I thought led back to the exit, but we ended up in the changing rooms. A dozen men and a couple of teenage boys were changing from their street clothes into white pants and shirts.

"Oops," I said. The folks at the front desk in the lobby hadn't checked for our recommends. We shouldn't have been able to get this far.

"We're going to get caught. We need to leave."

I looked at the men a moment longer. Train up a child in the way he should go, the proverb read, and when he is old, he will not depart from it. Perhaps that truism had more to do with brainwashing, though, than testimony.

I remembered when I was eight and my father baptized me. We'd had to change in the same room at the stake center. We entered the dressing room through the men's bathroom. I was mortified to have to change in front of my father, stripping down to my underwear, but it was worse after the baptism, when I had to change my wet underwear, too. Dad was so strong and masculine, and I was so puny. I was struck by the sight of his wet garments clinging to his buttocks.

I still liked looking at men in wet underwear. "Come on," I said, heading away. Ben followed.

We walked down the hall and around the corner, and suddenly we found ourselves on the edge of an endowment session. There wasn't even any door. The room opened right onto the hallway. We stopped and silently crept by. No one said anything, intent on listening to Michael/Adam.

"Royd," said Ben, "I want to get *out*."

"Me, too." There were no windows, so I couldn't see outside, and yet it was clear we must have somehow gone up some stairs without noticing. We obviously needed to go back down. I pointed to a stairwell, and we headed for the door.

"'We will go down,'" Ben said.

I snickered.

Down below, the temple was bustling with activity. There were several large rooms, again all without doors. One had a sign above it: McKinley Family Reunion. Another had a sign as well: Texas Houston Mission Reunion. The rooms were filled with people, and even more were roaming the halls.

"Oh, my god," moaned Ben. "We'll never get out of here."

"It'll be okay."

"Someone's going to catch on sooner or later."

"Let's try that hall over there."

We walked around a corner and had to descend more stairs. Now there were doors everywhere. Rich, heavy, dark wooden doors. One had the mission president's name on it. Another had the name of one of his counselors. There were half a dozen offices in sight.

"Oh, my god," Ben moaned again. "Why did you have to come in the temple?"

"I thought it would be fun to remember where we came from."

"Is it fun?" he asked.

"No," I admitted.

We kept walking and turned a corner. There, at the end of the hall, was a red EXIT sign. "Let's go!" I said. We hurried for the door.

It led to a stairwell, and we started climbing up again. At the top was a large room, like a foyer, only it wasn't the same lobby entrance where we'd entered earlier. There were again lots of people milling about, most in normal street clothes, not wearing white any longer as we were.

"There!" said Ben, pointing. "There's the door!"

We headed for it, but before we could reach it, we had to go through what looked like a subway turnstile. "It takes 75 cents," I said. "Do you have any change?"

"Oh my god."

We fumbled around in our pockets while people waited impatiently behind us and finally made it through the turnstile. Then we were at the door.

"We're underground," said Ben.

"But there's a ramp," I replied. "We can walk up to the surface."

"We'll get hit by a car." There were cars from an underground parking lot zooming up the ramp.

"I'll chance it," I said.

"Me, too," Ben agreed, nodding vigorously.

We started walking up the ramp, and someone behind us yelled for us to stop. We walked faster. Finally, we could see daylight. We just had to walk through one more set of glass doors, and we'd be free. Ben and I ran for the doors and pushed through.

We were now on a wide sidewalk, but it didn't seem to lead anywhere. There was no street, no other buildings, no people.

"We should have followed the cars," Ben said. "Let's go back in."

I pulled on the doors, but they wouldn't budge. I saw a sign: Holiness to the Lord.

I tried pushing on the doors instead, to no avail. I pulled again. "Ben, help me." We pushed and pulled together. We began beating on the doors, calling out. "Let us in! Let us in! Let us in!"

***

I sat up straight in bed, my forehead covered in sweat. Ben was lying beside me. He turned over. "You okay, Royd?" he whispered, putting his hand on my arm.

"I had the dream again," I said.

"The one about the temple?"

I nodded.

"It's because you saw that segment on the news about the man proposing to his boyfriend at the Salt Lake Home Depot. Those kinds of things always make you homesick."

"I'm scared." I held my arms tightly across my body.

"Here. Lie next to me." I did, and Ben snuggled up behind me. "It's okay," he whispered. "We're out now. It's okay." He wrapped his arm across my chest, and I tried to relax.

"Are we safe from them?" I asked.

"We're safe."

"But they're so powerful."

"We're safe." Ben hugged me close. I still had that after-nightmare dread, afraid to shut my eyes.

I could still see the temple, and ward meetinghouses, and stake centers. I could still see old men pointing fingers and shaking their heads. I could still see middle-aged women taking a plate of brownies away from me. I could still see young, carefree couples walking into the voting booth.

I felt Ben's arm on my chest and held it against me.

"In the morning," I whispered, "let's throw away the garments."

"Yes," he agreed softly, "it's time."

I snuggled backward more deeply into Ben's body and let out a deep sigh. I wished I knew why the Church still haunted me after all these years.

I closed my eyes and luxuriated in the warmth of my husband's love.

But why did I keep seeing the temple, even now, while I was awake? I sighed again, my hand on Ben's. Maybe in the morning, I'd get out my old triple combination and look for an answer.

Star Fleet Testing

I was mostly a lurker. Like an extra in the background from a scene set in Ten Forward, with Whoopi at the bar. An inappropriate comparison, I suppose, considering I didn't drink. But sometimes I was a lurker at church, too, watching as fathers blessed their babies and saw their sons and daughters off on missions. I felt I spent most of my life observing and not doing.

It had taken me years to bother looking at Facebook, and once I began, I still didn't feel the need to interact very often. People put up photos of their dog, or their mother's hat, or their newly polished bathroom doorknob. They went on at length about what they ate for lunch, or the long line at the bank, or what they thought of their neighbor's new drapes.

No one ever messaged me personally. The only interaction I managed was if a "friend" posted what was essentially an exceptionally brief diary entry and I felt the need to "like" it.

But millions of people related to each other in cyberspace and seemed to enjoy it, so perhaps I was being too close-minded. Nina and I long ago made a rule to eat dinner with the TV off, and even if we did watch a couple of shows later, we always set aside time to work together on a puzzle or plan a party for some of our friends from church or read to each other or do anything that would allow us to interact as participants and not as spectators.

And still I felt like a lurker most of the time.

While Nina and I didn't have any children of our own and probably never would now that we were in our early forties, all our friends in our Sacramento ward did. They frequently reminded us how unfortunate we were to be childless. Unable to fill the measure of our creation. Said with kindness, of course. As well as an air of superiority.

Because we didn't always relate to hours of talk about kid problems, we didn't get invited over to other people's houses very often, despite our own parties. People might shake my hand at church and then want nothing more to do with me. Unless it was time to ask for help on a service project. I would sit in the chapel every Sunday, watching Nina up on the stand directing music, see all the smiling faces dotted about the congregation, and feel utterly alone.

So I lurked. I suppose I was still hoping for a real connection somewhere, even if outside the Mormon universe. Nina and I helped raise funds for Elizabeth Warren. We collected money for the Red Cross. We helped give out food with Jewish Family Services. But while we might volunteer with other likeminded people, everyone usually focused on their job, not on becoming friends.

Nina didn't seem as bothered as I was. She'd just pick up a novel and read in bed while I headed back to Facebook. I'd dutifully go through everything posted, hoping for a reason to reach out, but try as I might, I consistently found myself unable to reply to anything.

"My friend Abigail's home was destroyed in a tornado last night," posted one friend from my old Single Adult group from twenty years ago. "She broke her arm and lost everything." I checked the latest comments submitted right before dinner. People seemed to post around the clock. The old Single Adult gang still kept in touch, though we were now scattered across the country. All the others had children by now, though a couple of folks from the gang were single once again.

"I'm so sorry for her loss," one person replied. "My prayers are with her."

"My condolences," wrote another.

"I send all my positive energy her way," said one more.

"All my love."

"I'll be praying for her."

"Sending my prayers to our wonderful Heavenly Father."

There were maybe fifteen responses in total, all much like these. Part of me felt astonished people could have so many friends, but something about the interaction still bothered me. I neglected to add my name to the list and signed off instead.

That night, Nina sat beside me on the sofa while we watched *Person of Interest*. "My feet hurt something awful tonight," she said. "Standing in new shoes at work all day."

"Put your lovely feet in my lap." She did and I began rubbing them as we continued watching the show.

"It's a fun series," Nina said, twitching her toes in pleasure, whether at the massage or the TV screen, I couldn't tell.

"I find it frustrating," I returned, nodding toward the set.

"Because…?"

"On the one hand, I see the importance of trying to focus your energy, but on the other, they're only getting numbers for one single person a week in a city of ten million, and they *aren't* getting numbers for anyone anywhere else in the country. Or the rest of the world, for that matter. It's like trying to save a beach from erosion, one grain of sand at a time."

"But it's interesting and exciting," she said.

"It *is* that," I agreed. Nina painted her toenails, though the two of us were the only ones who ever saw her toes. "And I suppose it teaches us the importance of taking a risk to help others."

"Not everything is a Sunday school lesson, Derek."

"I think sometimes Heavenly Father does talk to us through TV shows," I protested with a laugh. "When I was a kid, I watched this program called *Stingray*. It was about a man who went around helping people in trouble. He'd ask for favors from other folks he'd helped out earlier, in a kind of pay-it-forward fashion. I used to think Nick Mancuso was one of the Three Nephites."

"It's possible you watch too much TV."

"Ninety minutes a night, just like you, even as a kid."

"Maybe it's time to work on another puzzle." Nina clicked the remote, smiling as she led me to the puzzle table we'd set up near the window. "I bought a new one of the planet Earth from space. 1500 pieces."

"Too bad nobody else likes puzzles." I opened the box. My grandma had told me once that when she was a teenager, she and all her friends would get together on Sunday to put a puzzle together. It was a communal activity. "What do kids do these days?"

"We don't have to worry about what kids do these days." Nina started laying out all the pieces on the table.

"Shopping at the mall doesn't sound as meaningful."

"What's meaningful is doing something together, whatever it is."

I nodded and started looking for border pieces. They were all the color of space.

The following day at work, my supervisor, Suzanne, announced was quitting to start at a rival company for higher pay. While we'd all miss her, I also worried what jerk we might get in her place. Our department ordered two huge platters of Mexican food, but before we dug in, Suzanne gave a little speech, telling us all how much she'd miss us. Then she grabbed a huge cloth bag and began pulling items out.

"For you, Jen, because you have a heart the size of Texas…" Suzanne gave her a large stuffed red heart.

"For you, Margaret, because you always said you liked this scarf, it's yours now." She handed Margaret her favorite scarf.

"Bill, because you're a miserable sexist and always called me a doll, I give you this." She handed him a Barbie doll, and everyone laughed, except Jen, the girl with the large heart, who glared at him.

"Allen, because you're such a stuffed suit, I thought you could use these." She handed him a pair of brilliantly wild socks, half pink, half chartreuse, with lines and dots. He accepted them with an embarrassed smile.

Suzanne continued with her gifts, joking, "I think I've learned more about giving from *The Wizard of Oz* than from my pastor." After addressing a few more coworkers, she finally turned to me.

"Derek, because I hear you say such romantic things to your wife when you tell her you're on your way home, I give you this bottle of wine." I smiled as I admired the label, wondering if I should give it to our bishop at Tithing Settlement, since I "earned" it at work.

Soon we were all back at our desks. Why had Suzanne spent so much on us? It wasn't as if we were actually friends. Besides, if anything, we should all have been buying *her* gifts. Yet despite the frivolity, I could tell most of the staff felt touched by her efforts.

On Facebook that night, I noticed a post by someone from my mission group. "My aunt's home was flooded by a freak storm. Just the bottom floor, but she lost her best furniture. She's old and on Social Security. She has homeowner's insurance but not flood."

The responses were similar to those of the other night. "I'm so sorry for her loss!"

"I wish her the best!"

"My prayers are with her."

"I'll send good thoughts her way."

"Isn't that your aunt who left the Church?"

"It's the Last Days, you know."

"I'll pray for her."

"Maybe this will bring her back. It's really a blessing."

"God works in mysterious ways."

I didn't post a response.

Friday evening, Nina and I went to our monthly Star Trek meeting, the highlight of the month.

I wondered why Fast and Testimony meeting wasn't the highlight of each month.

Nina and I chatted with a former Catholic priest about how we'd create stars and planets of our own one day, hoping the Star Trek shows could give us some ideas. As nerdy as most of the attendees were, they could still be relatable in a way the Relief Society president wasn't. A few of the folks wore costumes and a couple of regulars played three-dimensional chess.

We watched the episode from Next Generation where Beverly finds that more and more crew members are disappearing. Afterward, we voted for the episode we wanted to see next month. The group chose the one where the young cadet who'd graduated with Wesley risks her life to atone for her behavior and ends up killed.

Then we played Star Trek trivia for half an hour.

No one here minded that we didn't have kids.

As the meeting drew to an end, Samuel came up to me. He was a pleasant guy in his mid-twenties who always wore Vulcan ears. "Derek, I'm going out of town next weekend. Would you be able to check in on my dog for a couple of days? He can get out in the back yard by himself through the doggie door, but he'll still want some attention and to go on a couple of walks."

"No problem, Sam."

"If you like," Nina interjected, "we could spend the weekend at your place and housesit, too. No charge."

"Really?"

"Sure. We like to have sex in other people's beds sometimes. So hard to do when you're married and Mormon."

Samuel laughed. I liked when Nina didn't hold back. Even if it wasn't a particularly clever remark, it was genuine. Unguarded.

The bishop's wife wouldn't have laughed.

"That bed's already seen lots of sleepovers," Samuel admitted with a smile. "A couple more bodies won't hurt. Just be sure to change the sheets before you leave."

"Not a problem. But if you have any Nutella around the house, for heaven's sake, hide it. Derek's a fiend."

"Nutella is an evil plot," I informed him, "sent from the future by Terminators to destroy the human race."

"Wrong show," Samuel said.

Saturday after weeding the garden, I went grocery shopping with Nina, and then we continued with our puzzle while listening to the radio. A radical environmentalist was making fun of the NGOs that had raised lots of money for conservation but didn't do anything drastic enough to make a difference. "They got almost 400,000 people to march around Central Park," the man complained, "but that was just a photo op. They didn't even march by the United Nations building. It's all show but no substance. The next day, a mere thousand protestors marched on Wall Street, to protest where the real problem is."

The speaker irritated me. There'd been no accompanying rally or march here in Sacramento. I gave regularly to the Sierra Club and the Nature Conservancy, though I'd recently read that the Nature Conservancy allowed oil drilling on some of their land, so maybe the guy had a point. I'd planted over six hundred trees with American Forests, though. I wondered how many trees the holier-than-thou protestor on the radio had planted. Or what *he'd* accomplished in limiting how much pollution corporations dumped into the world that those larger groups hadn't.

"Maybe next weekend when we dog-sit," Nina suggested, "we can go to the park, and while I tend to the dog, you can pull up some non-native species."

I inserted a piece of Africa into the puzzle.

"What difference can *I* make?" I asked. "The problems are too big. It'll take massive government intervention to save this planet."

"Big government?" Nina laughed. "Don't say that too loud or we'll get called before a Church court."

"I'm sure we're already on someone's list for being part of the Mormon Democrats Facebook group."

I inserted a piece of the Sahara desert.

Nina shrugged. "Doing the right thing doesn't always bring you friends." She held up a piece of the puzzle and wrinkled her nose as she considered where to place it.

Before getting ready for bed, I checked my Facebook feed again. Another of my old Single Adult friends had posted. This was from Shelly, who still lived here in Sacramento in a neighboring ward. "Just finished my first round of chemo. Doctors don't know if it'll help or not. I'm sick as a dog."

There were the usual responses. "My prayers are with you."

"I'll put your name on the temple prayer roll."

"I'm sending all my positive energy your way."

"God never gives us more than we can handle."

"It's a test. The Lord only tests those he believes in."

"Just remember that Heavenly Father loves you. We all love you."

"Keep going to church. You'll need the strength it gives you."

The futility of life suddenly struck me like a supernova. Even if every single life on Earth was important, we were still only one planet around a solitary star in a single galaxy. There were over *two hundred billion* other galaxies. It wasn't even possible to calculate the number of stars, much less planets, much less the life forms on those planets.

What could I do to help Shelly in any meaningful way? What could I do to fight political corruption? What could I do to save the environment? What could I do to cure Parkinson's? To end poverty? To stop war? Or human trafficking? Or child abuse? Or gang fighting? Or *anything*?

What could I do to develop enduring relationships, surely one of the most important tasks we faced on Earth, if life held any meaning at all?

I tried to think what my Church leaders would tell me, but as I looked at the responses from my fellow Mormons, I felt only disgust.

With friends like these…

Then a thought occurred to me from a recent Star Trek meeting. We'd watched my favorite Star Trek movie, *The Wrath of Khan*, and the idea of the Kobayashi Maru test had left a deep impression, though I'd seen the movie almost a dozen times before.

What if Earth life were *deliberately* a no-win situation? What if we *couldn't* solve any of the pressing problems of the world? What if it were *set up* that way on purpose? Perhaps it was all a character test, to see how we'd react to serious, grave emergencies, *knowing* we were going to lose.

I sometimes dreamed of winning the lottery, though as a Mormon, I wasn't even allowed to buy a ticket. But I thought about all the good I could do with a hundred million dollars. In reality, of course, I could win a billion dollars and it would still be almost useless. A hundred billion dollars. Four trillion dollars. And I *still* wouldn't have enough money to solve even a fraction of the world's problems. What good was my measly hundred million going to do?

Or the fifty dollars I actually had.

So many of the faithful felt that everything was in God's hands. They washed their own of almost every problem without a second thought. But Mr. Saavik didn't have the choice of passing off her Kobayashi Maru to a superior officer. It was *her* test. Passing the buck didn't show character.

I wondered why I didn't get lessons like this from the Book of Mormon. Or the temple ceremony.

Or General Conference.

I'd voted to watch the episode where Picard is zapped by a probe and lives an entire lifetime on a doomed planet. Perhaps Nina and I would watch it ourselves tomorrow. Certainly a better use of time than social media.

Shelly was sick and miserable.

So what *was* the answer to the Star Fleet test? Make a token effort? Do nothing at all?

Or do your very best, despite knowing the outcome?

Is that how one was eventually able to travel the star systems and inhabit other worlds?

I looked at Shelly's post once more and decided not to lurk any longer. Do *something*, I told myself. Do anything. "I'll be at your home tomorrow morning at 10:00 to take care of your laundry and vacuuming." I hit Enter, and then after thinking a moment, I added another line. "Oh, and my prayers are with you."

I logged out and went downstairs to tell Nina why I'd be skipping church in the morning. We hadn't missed a meeting in years. We felt we had to be extra diligent to make up for our childlessness.

But Nina smiled and put her hand on mine. "I'll clean the bathrooms while you vacuum," she said.

Maybe one good relationship was enough to leave this world with.

It was 10:30, our usual bedtime, but Nina nodded toward the puzzle table. "We're almost done," she said. "Let's finish putting the Earth together before we go to bed."

I kissed her and we sat back down. I picked up a piece of the ocean and looked for the empty space where it belonged.

Nudist Colonies in Heaven

Clare held Cassie's hand as they moved toward the head of the line. "I'm so afraid I'll forget what to say," Clare said nervously.

"It'll be okay," Cassie replied, patting Clare's hand. Cassie had been an abused wife back on Earth but had endured stoically and was now going to receive her reward. Clare had led an uneventful life but always magnified her Nursery callings. They'd met after they both died.

Clare took another step, shuffling forward in her white slippers. She was tired of the white jumpsuit. Surely, once past the veil, they could wear something more interesting. Clare imagined Celestial robes like those of the women from ancient Greece, or from the days of the Egyptian pharaohs, or maybe Japanese royalty. Some of those women would be going through the veil, too, she knew.

"Oh, Cassie, I know I'm going to forget."

"You passed Judgment Day, Clare. Just keep thinking about getting out of these jumpsuits. Everything is going to be fine."

Clare knew that Cassie was right. She'd always been a worrier, though, and spent most of her adult life longing for the peace that death might bring. Only it didn't bring any peace. She was the same person after she died she'd been before. Of course, she'd been sent to Paradise to wait for judgment, not Spirit Prison, so she'd known she had at least a fighting chance and could begin to relax a *little*.

Then, desperately wishing she had nails to bite, she'd suffered through Judgment Day, which in reality lasted some indeterminate and godawful length of time, and finally she was heading to the Celestial Kingdom. *With* nails, now that it was all over.

The top degree of heaven. The one where she would become a goddess.

Of course, she was thousands of years away from that, maybe millions. Right now, she was the same poor schlub she'd been in life. What she had now was opportunity, unlike her husband Baxter, who was going to spend eternity in the Terrestrial Kingdom. They'd been granted a temple divorce right after judgment.

When they reached the veil, Clare pushed Cassie ahead of her. She tried to eavesdrop to give herself a chance to review the things she'd have to say, but she couldn't make out their whispers. She had the handshakes down, though, so that wouldn't be a problem. Finally, it was her turn, and she pressed up against the white fabric.

She recited everything correctly, not even stumbling once. A hand reached for her and began to pull her through the veil. She felt lightheaded, as if she were being transported via a light tube, the way Moroni always showed up unannounced back in Paradise.

And suddenly, other hands were grabbing at her, too. She couldn't tell what was happening, but when she reached the other side, she realized her jumpsuit had been ripped off. She was standing next to Cassie naked. Cassie was naked, too, as were all the other people who'd just come through, most of them women.

"What the h—?" Clare began, stopping herself. She looked about and saw hundreds, maybe thousands, of people milling everywhere, going about their new lives in the Celestial Kingdom. Every one of them was naked.

A man walked up to them, flopping. "Welcome, sisters," he said. "This way, please."

Clare, Cassie, and several other women followed him. Clare wondered if she was supposed to be admiring his ass. She should probably exercise some restraint, she thought, but she reminded herself again she couldn't help but be the same person now she'd been when she died. Restraint might take a few thousand years. The man led them to a shuttle, and Clare watched through the window as they passed homes and shops in some Celestial city.

At least, they looked like shops, though certainly there would be no money up in the highest degree of heaven. She watched naked women walking their dogs, naked men handing fruit to other naked men, naked men and women singing together on a street corner. She couldn't quite place the architecture. Clare had never traveled much, but she watched TV all the time. These buildings didn't quite jive with any style she was familiar with.

But then, there'd been no TV all those years in Paradise, an oxymoron if ever there was one, so she might have forgotten such details. There were columns and reliefs and texture, and yet somehow none of the buildings impressed her very much. Perhaps she was just too shaken from the day's events. If she had to put a name on the style, she thought she might call it "Majestic Bland."

They reached a large marble structure and stopped. The boxy complex was several stories high and seemed to cover two city blocks. The flopping man opened the shuttle door, and then a bouncing woman ushered them off the vehicle. Several yards down, another vehicle dispersed naked people. Clare followed behind Cassie. To be honest, Cassie had a pretty nice ass herself. She supposed she did now, too.

Clare had never been the brightest LED in the world, but she got it. Adam and Eve had lived nude and without shame. If those in the highest degree of heaven weren't able to lead innocent lives now, when there was no longer temptation, would eternal life even be worth living?

The bouncing woman pointed to the building ahead of them. "This will be your home for the next little while. It's both a school and a dormitory. There are plenty of things to learn before moving to the next level of progression."

Clare raised her hand.

"Yes?"

"I thought we were already on the highest level."

The woman laughed. "If you live another trillion years, and you will, you'll always keep moving to higher levels. That's what it's all about."

Clare thought about the hokey pokey. She noticed there were no children anywhere. She raised her hand again.

"No kids until you become a goddess," the woman said. If she could read minds, Clare wondered why they were even bothering to speak. "And that could be eons away. Now let's get you settled in. Here are your packets." She handed them each a large blue folder.

Clare noticed a handsome black woman ahead of her in line. Beautiful, and wearing her skin proudly. She was the prettiest woman in line, without a doubt, sure to get a choice husband. Clare looked at her own pasty skin and then back at the woman. Perhaps black was the new black.

Clare and Cassie ended up as roommates, which delighted them both. "There are no sheets and blankets on the beds," Clare pointed out with a frown when they reached their room.

"Maybe it's because the temperature is always perfect," Cassie returned.

Clare shrugged, studying the ceiling, which also oddly seemed made of marble, making her feel as if she were living in a tomb. "I guess we should get settled in," she said. Then she laughed, setting her folder on her desk and then raising her empty hands.

They each had a bookshelf above their desks. Photographs were already pasted to the walls featuring various family members. Clare walked over to one of her sister Dinah. Underneath the photo was a schedule of Telestial Kingdom visiting hours. Other photos showed Samuel, Nathan, and Rebecca, Clare's three children who'd all left the Church years before she died. There was also a picture of her brother, Thomas, who'd actually seen Jesus and still abandoned the Church.

There'd be no visiting him in Outer Darkness. But there was a picture of Sally, the ward organist, who was down in the Terrestrial Kingdom while her husband was in the Telestial. Clare would need an Excel sheet to keep track of everyone. She wondered if she'd have to wear something when she went to the lower kingdoms, or if lesser beings just had to deal with their lust for her on their own. There didn't seem to be any closets in the room which might hold emergency garments. She'd just started rummaging through her desk drawers, which mostly seemed to contain pamphlets and study guides, when a loudspeaker crackled to life.

"Orientation in the auditorium in five minutes."

Cassie picked up a laminated card from her folder so she and Clare could study a map of the building. Bathrooms were at one end of the hall on their floor, a tiny kitchen at the other. A cafeteria was on the far side of the building, next to the auditorium.

They hurried out of the room, Clare pausing stupidly at the door until she realized she had no need to lock it. Almost two hundred people crowded into the auditorium, maybe a fifth of them men. Clare directed Cassie so they were sitting right behind two of them. Such lovely shoulder muscles. Resurrected bodies were to die for.

She laughed into her hand.

A tall, lanky man walked to the podium. Even from fifty feet away, Clare couldn't help but notice his member. She felt her nipples hardening and wished the new residents could at least have started out with green aprons and maybe moved up to complete nudity over a period of weeks or months.

"Welcome, cadets," the man began. Clare looked at Cassie and frowned. "You'll find that we keep very busy here. We have a variety of classes to help you learn and progress. Take just the ones you want, but realize that before you leave, you'll eventually have to take all of them. We have chemistry and physics, of course, and every language ever spoken. The languages alone will take you decades. But we have plenty of fun stuff, too."

Here he motioned for two assistants to hold up a large poster. The women's breasts pointed toward the main feature in the photo—a diploma. Clare couldn't help but focus on their pubic hairs glistening in the bright light.

She had a friend back in Relief Society who'd taken up the harp just in case she didn't make it to the top degree and had to settle for ministering angel. Clare didn't see Brenda anywhere, so apparently that had been a wise choice. Clare realized now that she and Baxter should probably have joined a nudist organization or at least gone to a few nude beaches to help prepare themselves for the afterlife.

"I wonder if I can volunteer to hold the sign next time," Cassie whispered.

It was a shame the women had to stand beside the man, Clare thought, and not behind him where at least they'd enjoy a better view.

"We have swim classes," the man continued. "Skinnydipping 101." He waited for the audience to laugh. How many times must he have given this speech? Clearly, lots of the people on this side of the veil had been here for quite some time. Clare had always been told time had no meaning in heaven. Perhaps there was some way the entrance was staggered for all the newbies.

"And we have skin painting. Of course, you'll get both to model and learn painting and sculpture using each other as models. You must learn every single talent sooner or later. There's no becoming a god or goddess without knowing *everything*. So we have yoga and gymnastics and ballroom dancing." He motioned for the assistants to walk off with their sign. "You name it, we teach it."

The talk went on and on. Clearly, the man hadn't learned yet how not to be boring. It would undoubtedly be a good while longer before he became a god himself.

"Finally," the man said, "we do some things just for fun. We have dances and singalongs and arm wrestling and volleyball." Clare looked at Cassie. "And…" he dragged out the sentence, waiting for everyone to give him their complete attention, "the activity I know you'll all enjoy—Speed Dating." He laughed. "Come on out here, guys!"

Now several men walked onto the stage. "I picked these guys out myself as the shuttles arrived to give you a taste of what it'll be like. It'll be ages before you can have kids, of course, but these men need helpmeets now."

Clare wondered if they were all divorced, or if their wives hadn't passed judgment. Perhaps they were celibate gay men who'd now turned straight or guys already married looking for more wives. "I assume you gals found your IUDs in your welcome folders. Naturally, you won't need them until after the Speed Dating." He chuckled. "All the women will stop at a table with each man, and everyone will get a feel for each other. At the end of the activity, we'll see if anyone wants to pair up. We'll keep holding the event every Friday until everyone is matched up. It's not as if any one of these guys won't make a perfect husband. We'll all deity material here."

He waved to the men, asking each to step forward as their name was called. "Jeff. Felipe. Clark. Abiola. Tyrell. Yoshi. Farouk. Ivan. Spencer." Odd how every man there had a perfect body, Clare thought, and yet some were still more beautiful than others. The speaker started clapping, and soon everyone in the audience joined in. The men bowed and jogged off stage.

That flopping was distracting. Clare turned to look about the auditorium. How many of these women were going to end up her sister wives? She grabbed Cassie's hand. Cassie held on tightly in return.

The speaker ushered a new woman out to the podium to finish the presentation. "We don't want to overwhelm you on the first day," she said with a smile, "so this afternoon, we'll have a picnic out on the quad, and then you'll have free time the rest of the day. Classes begin tomorrow at 7:00 a.m." She clapped her hands twice, and everyone stood to leave.

As they flowed out into the halls, Clare noticed that the water fountains along the walls seemed to be placed awfully low, forcing people to bend over quite far. That looked like Tyrell sipping some water now. Clare went to stand behind him in line. "You were great on stage," she said when he turned away from the fountain.

"Thanks," he said with a wink.

Clare took her sip and then joined Cassie again. She kept thinking of Louis Armstrong's "Wonderful World." Back in their dorm room, they both sat on their respective beds and looked about the room. "Two more hours until the picnic," Cassie said. She caught herself twiddling her thumbs and stopped.

Clare nodded. She wanted to take a nap. They hadn't done much today, but she still felt wiped out. A body was a body, after all, even a perfect one.

What did perfect even mean, if one still had to eat and sleep and defecate?

The questions exhausted Clare even more. She wanted to lie down, but back on Earth she'd always needed the weight of a blanket, even in the summertime, to feel comfortable enough to relax. She looked over at Cassie, who seemed just as lost as she felt. "Will you lie on top of me for a while?" Clare asked her.

She had no idea how the woman would react to such a request. They'd never known each other back when they had mortal bodies, after all. But Cassie nodded and joined Clare on her mattress. Clare lay down, and Cassie rested her body gently on top of hers.

Clare wrapped both arms across Cassie's back with a heavy sigh and then closed her eyes, thinking of Baxter and Dinah. She thought about Samuel and Nathan and Rebecca, and about Sally and Thomas, and all the others she loved who were banned from her life, and tried to fall asleep.

Going-Out-Of-Religion Sale

"Melissa, are you sure you want to do this?"

"Raise the garage door, Adam."

My husband pushed a button, and the garage door slowly opened. It was a bright, sunny morning in mid-April, and Mt. Olympus was as stunning as ever. I was still glad to be in Salt Lake, even if I didn't have much of a social life to look forward to any longer. I felt too angry around people, especially devout Mormons. But I had to go through with this.

I started lugging the heavy boxes of books, and Adam joined in reluctantly. We set up two card tables and placed the other objects we'd be selling on top. Still more objects had to rest on the pavement. I set up two folding chairs for when we needed to take a break. By 6:30, everything was ready. We'd said in our ad the garage sale started at 8:00, but of course, even before 7:30, people were already driving up.

"Good morning, Sister Vanderveer," our first visitor said cheerily. Sister Hoffmann attended Relief Society in my ward. Or rather, in my former ward. I expected people to come from all over Salt Lake today, given the possibility of finding good stuff at a Mt. Olympus address, but it was only natural my neighbors stop by as well.

"Enjoying your morning walk?" I returned. Sister Hoffmann had diabetes. I wished I'd put my ten-pound weights out to sell, but I was still using them myself. While I felt consumed with anger, it wasn't specifically toward *her*.

"I…" Sister Hoffmann's voice trailed off as she assessed our sale items. She turned to me with a puzzled expression. She stole a glance at Adam, who smiled back uncertainly.

"You've always liked that framed print of the Nauvoo temple," I said. "The price is pretty low."

Sister Hoffmann's brows furrowed. She sputtered something incoherent and hurried off.

"Told you," said Adam.

"Fuck her," I said, angry again. "She'll be back. And she'll bring half the ward with her."

"I still think we should have donated this stuff to Deseret Industries."

"Adam, how much have you paid in tithing over the past twenty-five years?"

He paused and did some mental calculations. "At least $300,000," he said wearily.

I nodded. "The last thing I'm going to do is give another penny to the Church."

A few people stopped by I didn't recognize. They too gave me odd looks, but they bought three Church books and a framed photo of the First Presidency. Someone else picked up the framed Proclamation on the Family. A woman gasped upon seeing the box of garments. We were only selling underwear still in its packaging, of course, but the woman actually ducked, looking up to the heavens as if expecting lightning to strike. The skies were clear. Maybe we'd go on a hike tomorrow.

Adam lowered his head and covered his face. "This is going to be a long day."

"Hold your head up," I told him.

"Melissa, we don't have to do this in public. Why couldn't we just stop attending? Why do we need to make such a fuss?"

I thought of the countless hours I'd spent in Sacrament meeting, in Relief Society, teaching the Young Women, teaching Primary. I thought of all the crafts I'd done, the baking, the emails I'd written to Brian and Rebecca on their missions. I thought of all the hours I'd spent cleaning the ward bathrooms, vacuuming up Cheerios in the chapel. And I thought of all the times Adam's parents had refused to visit because they had to go to the temple.

His folks lived in St. George and hadn't come to see even one of our three children when they were born. They didn't come to either Brian or Rebecca's mission farewells. Or homecomings. They felt their time was better spent watching the damn temple movie for the three hundredth time, because our dead ancestors were more important than their living descendants. They treated the other kids and grandkids the same, and no one else in the family seemed to mind.

I minded.

But that wasn't the worst. What pushed me over the edge were the mission accounts. When the kids were born, Adam's parents opened bank accounts for all three and began donating funds on every birthday and on Christmas. The children never received a single toy or gift. Only contributions to their funds. And it was made clear right from the start that if the kids didn't go on a mission, Adam's parents would take the money back.

Conditional money. Conditional love. Conditional salvation. And all the conditions could never *really* be met. Adam's parents had withheld the last $200 from Brian's account because he didn't make zone leader.

There was no doubt the rest of the funds had been a big help when Brian served in South Africa and Rebecca was called to Ireland, but this past year, Shawn told us he had no intention of going on a mission himself. He wanted to focus all his energy on a Political Science degree and then a Masters' in Social Work.

"And there aren't many scholarships in those fields," he pointed out. "I already asked Gram and Gramps if I could use the money from the account. They said they'd think about it." But a week later, we received a statement in the mail showing the account had been closed. That was two weeks ago.

It wasn't as if Adam and I couldn't afford to send Shawn to college, though using those funds would certainly have been nice. It was the slow, dawning recognition I'd been manipulated my entire life. Adam had even lost fifty thousand dollars in an affinity fraud scheme that wiped out our former bishop and a couple of other ward members. But fifty thousand dollars was nothing compared to what we'd willingly given in tithing and other contributions to the Church itself.

I wondered if that was a form of affinity fraud, too.

"Adam, we're doing this publicly because the Church *depends* on us to do it quietly."

"But…"

"If you want to go inside, I understand."

Adam sighed but didn't move.

I thought about sending a card to Adam's parents on their next wedding anniversary, announcing we were following their example and no longer gifting them directly but donating to charity in their name. Perhaps I could include a receipt to the homeless shelter downtown for gay teens. Or Planned Parenthood. Or to Everytown. I smiled.

Being angry was oddly satisfying. Yet oddly unsatisfying as well.

Sister Thorndyke walked up to the driveway a few minutes later with Sister Bonamy. "Good morning," I said in my cheeriest voice. They looked at me guardedly, clearly having been forewarned. They looked through the four boxes of Church books, studied the sculpture of two praying hands, and one of Joseph Smith kneeling. But when they reached the box of white robes and green aprons, even their advance knowledge couldn't keep them from gasping.

"What…what are you *doing*?" Sister Bonamy spluttered. "What…what…?"

"I'm having a Going-Out-Of-Religion sale."

"You're going to Outer Darkness!" Sister Thorndyke corrected me.

"How…how do you feel?" Sister Bonamy asked. She looked as if she expected sores to pop out suddenly on my forehead. I stole a glance at Adam.

"Happier than I've ever felt in my entire life."

The two women looked at each other. "That makes me so sad," said Sister Bonamy.

"Well, this is about you, isn't it?"

"Let's get out of here," said Sister Thorndyke, pulling on her friend's arm.

Sister Bonamy nodded but removed Sister Thorndyke's hand. "I want to get those Motab CDs first."

After she made the purchase, she rejoined Sister Thorndyke on the sidewalk, who offered in her kindest voice, "We'll pray every day that Heavenly Father sends you plenty of afflictions to help you repent."

The Mormon Security Guard God.

"I wish only the best for you, too." I said it as sincerely as I could manage. I didn't hate these women, despite what they said, despite my anger. I understood them. It was true I'd been growing disenchanted with my friendships at church the past few years, since we never seemed able to talk about the things which bothered or worried me most.

When Sister Cadow began showing up with bruises she was too embarrassed to talk about, we accepted her explanations without pressing. It was only when her husband finally broke her jaw that it all came out. Instead of rallying around her, half the women in the ward pulled away, too uncomfortable with real life to deal with it.

I'd been one of those women. Even while I had secrets of my own I couldn't share. The herpes Adam gave me. Or the growing suspicion Shawn was gay. Church became more and more suffocating.

"What's in this box?" asked a woman with a small child in tow. She pointed to a metal lockbox. She tugged at the lid but the box was locked on purpose.

"My signs and tokens," I replied. "Ten dollars."

The woman looked at me in confusion and walked away. I sometimes forgot there were non-members in Salt Lake. I'd be one of them soon. Adam and I had mailed our resignation letters yesterday. Notarized.

As the morning drew on, most of the books and artwork and garments disappeared. Someone even bought the temple clothing. We'd probably sell the last of the items by 1:00. I carried one of the tables back into the garage. Adam stopped looking nervous, which was just as well since there was no going back at this point. Everyone knew. One woman put her hand on my arm and said gently, "Why didn't you talk to me?"

I wanted to tell her it was because every time I attempted to, she changed the subject. But as all the Mormon material faded out of our lives, so did some of my anger. "I'm happy to talk to *you* any time," I said softly. I knew she was having trouble with one of her sons, though it wasn't clear exactly what was going on. For obvious reasons. "You want to stop by after church tomorrow?"

"Oh…I…I'll think about it. You have a good day, Sister Vanderveer. You, too, Brother Vanderveer." She walked off down the street, glancing over her shoulder once and then turning away quickly when she saw I was watching her. I felt another flash of anger. Maybe I was being a bitch ending things this way. If I was leaving the Church, I should leave passive aggressiveness behind as well.

"Uh-oh," Adam said quietly.

"What is it?"

He pointed, and I could see Bishop Steinbach heading our way, wearing pressed jeans and a heavily starched shirt. "Good morning, Melissa," he said. "Good morning, Adam." I marveled at the use of our first names. He looked about at the few remaining books and the sole remaining packaged pair of garments.

"Good morning to you, too," I replied. "I'm sorry about all this." I motioned to the driveway. Bishop Steinbach had always been kind to me. I felt suddenly as if I'd signed the divorce papers I'd drawn up after Adam's affair only to realize too late I'd made a bigger mistake than he had. Fortunately, I'd caught myself in time to work things out with him. Perhaps I'd acted too quickly with the Church as well.

But the Church's betrayal felt far deeper than anything Adam had done.

"I was wondering, Melissa," he began, looking me steadfastly in the eye. "I was wondering if you'd accept one last calling before you leave. I'd like you to give a talk next Sunday. Not tomorrow. A week from tomorrow."

My mouth fell open.

"Are you fucking kidding me?" Adam walked over toward us. "Are you *still* being a member missionary? That's the rudest fucking thing—"

Bishop Steinbach held up a hand. "Melissa, you've always been a good speaker in Sacrament meeting. The truth is I want out, too. But I could never say over the pulpit what I need to say. My counselors would pull me away from the microphone as soon as they saw where the talk was heading."

"And they'll let *me* talk?" I asked, trying to regain my composure.

"They'll see I'm condoning it, and that will delay their reaction a bit. You'll get further in your talk than I would."

"What am I going to say?"

"You'll tell everyone about your journey," he said simply.

I looked at Adam, and he looked back in confusion. The idea was tempting, but since everyone in the ward must surely know about my apostasy by now, I wasn't at all sure it would work. Besides, I wasn't leaving for any historical or theological reasons, only because of Mormon culture. And I'd said what I had to say by having my garage sale. I was done.

"Bishop," I said, "I think that's a talk you have to give."

He shook his head. "My wife won't allow it. She's ready to leave, too, but she doesn't want to be mean about it."

Adam put his hand on the bishop's arm. "The Church depends on people going quietly," he said, giving me a small smile.

The man sighed. "I guess they're right. I'm so worn out all I want to do is get it over with. I don't want to fight anymore. I've been fighting inside so much I've beaten myself to a pulp."

Adam and I looked at each other. The bishop still had two teens at home. It was bad enough when we told Brian and Rebecca, who both freaked out, but at least they were away living on their own. The bishop might have to deal with two unhappy teenagers for several more years. Teens didn't handle being outcasts very well. Perhaps it was unfair to make them try.

"Why don't you and Maureen come over for dinner tomorrow night?" I asked. "The kids can fend for themselves for one meal."

"What'll we do?" he asked. "What'll we talk about? Do we even have anything in common besides being Mormon?"

"We'll find out," I said. "We'll talk about our hobbies, about TV shows or movies we've seen. About politics. About anything other than the Church."

"It'll be strange," the bishop said slowly.

I laughed. "There are billions and billions of people out there who hold conversations every day that have nothing to do with the Book of Mormon. I'm sure we can, too."

"I'll ask Maureen."

Adam went to retrieve the "Free" sign we'd made last night, and he put the remaining few items on the sidewalk, placing the sign on top. I'd also made a sign that added "But Costly" but decided not to add it to the pile, after all. Bishop Steinbach helped us carry the last table and the two chairs back into the garage.

I felt as if I'd just lost ten pounds. Well, I *had* lost ten pounds since Adam's affair. He'd lost fifteen pounds himself. Strange how something awful could lead to something good. Bishop Steinbach started to leave, and I thought now might be a good time to try that cookie recipe Sister Bonamy had given me a few weeks ago.

I looked at Adam, then looked back out to the sidewalk. Instead, we invited the bishop in for a drink.

Putting on a Show

One day, when I step up on stage to accept my Academy Award, I'll tell everyone about my first big acting job. Sure, I'd been a member of the Drama Club in my Sandy high school, and I'd acted in two plays my first year at the University of Utah, but it was my performance as a Mormon missionary that really gave me the experience necessary to eventually earn a nomination. It started when I intercepted the mailman.

"Where are you going, Porter?" Megan, my best friend, strained to get a peek as I opened the envelope in her off-campus apartment. I still lived at home but didn't want to open the mission call there.

I read the letter. "Tulsa, Oklahoma," I replied.

"You can't be serious."

I shrugged. We brought the letter to a print shop in downtown Salt Lake and had a new page printed with an identical letterhead. This was back in 1982, I should point out, well before people could do this kind of thing on their PCs. The printer didn't bat an eye, and the next day, I picked up the sheet and brought it back to Megan's. She was a better typist and imitated the wording on the original letter. The only difference was that now my call was to the Italy Rome mission.

"You'll never get away with this," Megan said, shaking her head.

"When I was ten," I replied, "I convinced my parents a raccoon had gotten into the house and eaten all the cookies in the cookie jar."

"In Sandy?" Megan laughed.

"And when I was fifteen, I convinced my parents someone must have dented the front fender while the car was sitting parked in the driveway."

Perhaps the biggest hurdle was impersonating the bishop when I called the Tulsa mission president and explained that young Elder Simpson had decided against serving a mission after all. I had considered only pretending to send in my application, but as it was the bishop who did the actual sending, there was no way out of it. I explained to the mission president I'd already had a serious talk with both the young elder and his parents. I kept my fingers crossed, hoping there'd be no follow up calls. This could all unravel quickly.

"You're going to the Telestial Kingdom, you know," Megan stated matter-of-factly.

I nodded. While I didn't want to serve two years as a Mormon missionary, I did still believe the Church was true. Meaning I knew I'd have to repent of my deception one day.

But that day was not yet. I'd been working summer jobs at Dairy Queen since I turned sixteen three years earlier, and I'd mowed lawns for a couple of years before that. My dad made me put all the money in a special savings account in his name, so it wasn't as if I could just access it whenever I wanted. I didn't tell him I also got a campus job this past year and put all that money into my own account at another bank.

$2000 wouldn't go far, but it would pay for the plane ticket to and from Italy. Normally, the Church paid air fare for missionaries, but while I might be able to fake a mission for my parents, there was no way to fake it for the Church. I'd have to pay for the tickets myself. But Dad could supplement my daily living expenses in Italy from the mission savings account.

If I could convince him I was actually on a mission.

"Elder Simpson," Dad said in a thick voice as he dropped me off in front of the Missionary Training Center in Provo, "make me proud." He hugged me and wiped away a tear. Mom had too many tears to wipe away. I was her first-born, after all. I felt like a heel, but hours of endless talks hadn't swayed their position. I had to serve a mission.

It reminded me of a senior I knew at the U. Anita's parents would only pay for her degree if she studied Education. She made it all the way to her last semester in Chemistry before they discovered the truth. I wondered how far I'd make it. I wanted at least a month in Rome. That would still be the most incredible experience I was ever likely to have.

I headed for the front door of the main building of the missionary complex wearing my suit and tie, carrying my two suitcases. Once inside, I turned and looked back until my parents drove away. Then I went back out and waited for Megan. She picked me up in her ratty blue car with the gray door and we drove to Salt Lake. I stayed with her the next two months until time to leave for the mission field.

Staying with her was a bit problematic, of course. She couldn't invite friends over who might gossip. And I couldn't leave the apartment and risk being seen at the store by someone from my ward. So I did what any good Mormon boy in my position would do. I studied Italian six hours a day and read Shakespeare during the rest. I did want to be an actor, after all, when I "grew up."

Megan was also a good Mormon, so nothing ever happened between us. She even went so far as to recount her Sunday School lessons to me when she came home from church. "We can't let a missionary go completely inactive," she explained.

"Please don't see me off at the airport," I wrote to my mom just before the big day. "It isn't fair to the other missionaries whose parents don't live as close." I'd already asked my parents not to write me while I was at the MTC. "It'll make it harder for me," I said. "But I'll give you my address in Italy."

One bullet dodged. Or maybe it was sixty. Every day seemed like its own bullet. All this work and I hadn't accomplished anything more than hang out in Megan's apartment. But finally I was on my way to Rome. I wore my suit to the airport just in case someone we knew spotted me. I'd even had a nametag made up at the printer's shop. Once in Italy, though, I was on my own.

I found a small apartment near Tuscolano. It cost way more than the $250 a month missionaries were supposed to get from home. I still had a little left over in my personal account, but it wouldn't last long, and I had to save some of it for the return ticket. After unpacking, I walked down to the street and into a tiny pizzeria that sold pizza by the slice.

"Quanto pagate di solito per un impiegato?" I asked.

"We're not hiring," the man behind the counter replied.

"I'll take half pay," I said, "plus work one hour off the clock each day." I paused. "For the first week." Even that offer made me feel a bit like a scab. But desperate people did desperate things.

He frowned and then called to his wife in back. They talked a few moments before the man turned to me and nodded. Even at the bargain price, the couple could only hire me four days a week. But I was soon taking the shifts they didn't want and feeling as secure as anyone could at a job with no guarantees.

One day each week, I taught English lessons at the university for free in exchange for free Italian lessons. I never made the least effort to find the local LDS branches, opting instead to spend an hour on Sundays in the nearby Catholic church to get even more exposure to the language.

But this was only the beginning. Over the next several months, I managed to make friends with folks in three different parts of Rome. I'd have my parents send mail first to my real address, then to an address in northeast Rome, then to an address in southwest Rome, then to an address in northwest Rome, and then to my real address again. An actual missionary would be stationed in other cities in the mission, but trekking across town once a week to pick up mail was a big enough pain as it was. I could hardly take the train to Naples once a week, or the ferry to Sardinia.

And so life went on. I became rather proficient at pizza making, learned every verb tense, and still got to see some of the sights. I had Marco, my best bud, take pictures of me in my suit and nametag in front of the Coliseum and Vatican, and in my "P-Day clothes" up in Castel Gandolfo. I made up stories about conversions, disappointments as investigators changed their minds, arguments with companions, and whatever else I could think of.

I'd never wanted to do Improv, and since I had time to think out my letters, I suppose even this didn't count, but I read a lot of Pirandello to keep my acting goals in mind. Marco and I went to the occasional play, but even the cheap ones were usually more than we could afford very often.

Then came a day that almost destroyed the whole thing. It was 9:00 in the evening, and I'd gotten off work at 8:30. I was alone in my apartment and had just pulled off my shirt when I heard a knock at the door. I looked through the peephole and saw two young men in suits.

Oh, my heck, I thought. I'd been found out.

I quickly threw my shirt back on over my garments and opened the door with a smile. "Sí?" I asked innocently.

"Buona sera," said the younger looking of the two elders. "Siamo rappresentanti della Chiesa di Gesú Cristo dei Santi degli Ultimi Giorni." His accent was awful.

"Sí?" I repeated.

"We have a message about Jesus Christ we'd like to share with you and your family," the other elder continued in Italian, his accent slightly better. "Do you have a few minutes?"

They were tracting me out. I looked at them a long moment as they exchanged nervous glances. Finally, I shook my head and smiled. "I was born Catholic, and I'm going to die Catholic." I started closing the door.

"Here's our card in case you change your mind." The senior companion thrust it at me. I took it and locked the door, leaning against it with a sigh of relief. Then I heard a knock at the door one apartment over.

I'd definitely made the right decision.

I continued to get better at making pizzas, and I worked on improving my own accent. But a life of sin couldn't keep my soul untainted forever. I eventually broke down and tried espresso. And then one degenerate day, even a glass of wine.

I would be excommunicated when the story came out in the end. And it always did. Every play I'd ever read or movie I'd ever seen with this kind of deception always ended badly.

At least I never tried cigarettes. In Italy, that was saying something.

Once a month, I went to the one bank which allowed me to retrieve $250 from my mission savings account, and I began looking for a better job that paid more. I continued getting letters from home and making stuff up as I wrote back. I kept copies of my own letters so I could keep track of my fabrications. Anita wrote that she was finishing her graduate degree in Chemistry, having earned a scholarship. Megan was a semester away from earning her BA in English.

My own career was stalled, inevitable given the circumstances, but I was at least having a good time and learning a little about the world. Once, taking out the pizzeria owners' niece, I even copped a feel. Another time, while we kissed on the grass in the Villa Torlonia, she was the one to cop a feel.

This had to be better than talking to people about the Church.

Laura and I eventually broke up when she met someone else, but life was still grand. I might actually pull this off, I realized.

I'd been on my mission eighteen months when all Outer Darkness broke loose.

It was a Sunday, I wasn't working at the pizzeria and was just relaxing, reading another Italian play. There was a knock at the door. I saw two more elders in suits in the stairwell and thought about simply pretending I wasn't home. But I wouldn't have wanted someone to treat me like that, so I opened up.

"Chi é?" I asked.

"Cut the crap, Elder Simpson," said the taller of the two elders in English. His nametag said Anziano Snow. "We know what's going on."

Porca la miseria. "What are you talking about?" I spluttered, realizing too late I'd just spoken in English and given myself away in any event.

"Do you know a Roger Talbot?" Elder Snow demanded.

I frowned.

"Yeah. From your ward. He just arrived in the mission as a greenie two days ago." He looked me up and down as if expecting to see lice crawling over my body. "You can imagine his surprise when he found out no one had ever heard of you."

Well, there's no sense in belaboring the point. My dad cut off all the rest of the funds I'd earned, and the job at the pizzeria was no longer enough to pay the bills. I had enough left in my own account to buy a ticket back home, but I couldn't think of anything I'd rather do less. I asked Marco to light a candle for me, and I fasted for the first time since I arrived in Italy.

"Please, Heavenly Father," I prayed, "I know I should do the right thing, but I want to stay in Rome. I want to be an actor. I want to win the Coppa Volpi."

I fasted a full forty-eight hours, and nothing happened. But I still didn't want to go back to Salt Lake. Even though no one had responded to my job application at Cinecittá, I decided to go to the studio in person. Again, I won't belabor the point, but I got a job that day working on the food crew. That was how I first met Valeria.

We've been married over thirty years now, have two grown sons and a daughter just finishing university. We've raised them all minimally Catholic, just enough to feel part of the culture but not so much they suffer guilt at every turn. My parents never have come to visit, and life certainly didn't turn out as I'd hoped. I've acted in small roles in over a dozen films, have performed bigger roles on stage in a few local productions, but now, at the age of fifty-three, I'm still waiting to be discovered.

But whether I ever win an award or not, the work I'm most proud of is being a husband and father to an Italian family. It turns out that role doesn't require any acting at all.

Santa's Wedding Banquet

I didn't feel very jolly.

I stood at the bus stop on Renton Avenue South, waiting for the 106 to take me downtown for my interview at Carlyle's clothing store. I no longer wanted to be Santa, but what else was I going to do?

A brisk wind blew against my face, drying out my eyes. I hoped the cold turned my cheeks red. It was only early November in Seattle, so the temperature was right around 45 degrees. I was still wearing my light jacket.

The bus pulled up. As it did so, I peered through the windows to see if anyone was trying to exit through the front. I didn't notice any movement, but after the driver opened the doors, she pushed the button that lowered the front of the bus, clearly indicating someone elderly or disabled was about to exit. I waited for the beeping to end but still didn't see anyone coming toward the door.

Then the driver waved me aboard, and I realized *I* was the decrepit old person she'd lowered the front of the bus for. I climbed aboard and tapped my Orca card against the reader. The driver smiled pleasantly at me.

"Bitch," I thought, walking to my seat.

I'd turned sixty-five the week before and registered immediately for Social Security. The same day, I applied for the Santa position. I figured it would be a fun way to ease into retirement. Quirky and light-hearted. That was me.

Elaine hadn't been impressed. "You quit your job?" she shrieked. "Right before our wedding?"

"Now I'll have more time to spend with you," I replied. "We can go on walks, take little trips, do things together."

"But your Social Security won't be nearly enough to support me! Barry, what were you thinking?" She was thirty-five with no children but still receiving alimony from her non-member ex-husband. She'd been so beautiful at the Singles dance where I first saw her three months ago, with shoulder-length blond hair and green eyes. And she looked more beautiful every time I saw her.

After we played miniature golf in the rain, I treated her to hot chocolate and a warm blanket in my kitchen. I loved the easygoing way she laughed when I took her to a Russian film festival without subtitles. I'd brought her more and more exotic flowers for each date, until she said she'd rather I save up and buy her something beautiful and permanent. Her birthstone was emerald, she informed me.

Four days after I told her about retiring, she canceled the wedding. We were supposed to marry in the Bellevue temple tomorrow. She was a convert, so no one in her family was coming inside with us. My only daughter, Carolyn, was inactive and no longer paying her tithing, so no one on my side was allowed to participate, either.

I wondered if Janice would've come. Did the guards in Spirit Prison let the spirits of first spouses into the temple? Janice had been inactive her last few years before she died a decade ago, but she'd always brought food to our neighbors when they were sick.

I watched as a stout Latina carrying a bundled baby climbed on board in Hillman City. A three-year-old girl dragging a torn blue blanket trailed behind her.

They'd be too poor to have their picture taken with Santa.

Too poor.

Elaine had insisted I rent an expensive hall in Renton and invite all the "important" people from both our wards, plus all her extended family. I'd asked Carolyn and her two kids to come as well. Carolyn was divorced and not seeing anyone at the moment, not even a non-member.

Her two boys were both in college and could probably use a good meal. Neither had served a mission, but they still came to my house every few weeks and took care of my lawn, refusing any money in return, though I certainly could have afforded to pay them.

Even living on Social Security wasn't going to be the sacrifice Elaine seemed to think it was. Of course, the cost of the hall and the 120 dinners was beyond reason, but I wanted to make Elaine happy. Ten years was a long time to stay celibate. Since everything was already paid for at this point, I'd now have 120 guests and no bride.

Wouldn't that be fun.

I walked off the bus at Westlake and made my way up to street level. A man with a scraggly beard thrust a dirty McDonald's cup at me. I ignored him and continued on to Carlyle's. The street was busy with shoppers.

Janice had always liked Carlyle's. I'd brought her to pick out the prettiest outfit she could find every Christmas. But I'd still always added a special surprise under the Christmas tree. She left greeting cards for me all year round which I'd find propped against my monitor when I came home from work.

Any occasion would do. There were cards for St. Patrick's Day and Bastille Day, but there were also cards for Homemade Bread Day and for Clean Out Your Refrigerator Day.

I remembered a Halloween card she gave me once, with a yard full of jack o' lanterns on the front. Inside, she'd written, "Monsters don't scare me. Ghosts don't scare me. The only thing I find frightening is the thought of being without you." She bought me a T-shirt covered with pumpkins to wear when I handed out candy to the neighborhood kids. She refused to ever wear a T-shirt herself, feeling too self-conscious.

"It's not fair for me to be the one wearing the pumpkin patch," I told her, "when *you're* the Great Pumpkin who brings joy to everyone." Then I'd worried she thought I was referring to her stomach. I'd given her a long, passionate kiss, hoping to make up for it, and the following week, I enlarged a recent photo of her and had it framed so I could hang it in the living room.

I'd put it in my closet two weeks after starting to date Elaine.

I looked up now at the massive store which covered an entire downtown block. Would every mannequin on display remind me of Janice at Christmas?

Well, given that she'd weighed two hundred pounds at the end, it wasn't likely. But really, I was like *Shallow Hal*. Janice had always looked beautiful to me, even after the stroke which left her face contorted the last two days of her life. Of course, Elaine had looked beautiful, too. Though she'd never be able to wear that low-cut green dress again after going through the temple.

Taking a deep breath, I entered the building and headed for Men's Shoes, where Amanda from HR had asked me to meet her. I was a few minutes early and sat by the elevators. A man with his nine-year-old daughter walked by. He was heading for the escalators. The girl pointed to the elevators instead.

"Dad! Dad! Why can't we take the elevators?"

"Come on, Claire."

"But I want the elevators!"

Elaine had insisted on a limousine to take us from the temple to the reception hall.

The dad waved the girl over. She muttered in protest the entire way.

I looked at my watch and walked the rest of the way over to Men's Shoes. "I'm here to meet Amanda at 10:00," I said.

A well-dressed young man with his sideburns cut into a V nodded and went behind a curtain. A few moments later, a young woman walked out. She could hardly be much over eighteen.

"Barry?" she said, holding out her hand. "I'm Amanda."

"Pleased to meet you."

"Let's go over to Starbucks and have a chat about Santa." She smiled, and I followed her out of the store and across the street.

Amanda ordered something with the word "Americano" in it, and I ordered a cup of milk. We sat at one of the tables.

"So Barry, why do you want to be Santa?" she asked.

I closed my eyes for a second. "It seemed like a fun way to spend the holidays," I said slowly. I took a sip of my milk and then looked down at a tiny bubble.

"We get a lot of kids," she went on. "The line can be five or six hours."

"Really?" Janice had given me steamed milk before bed on the weekends, always a treat. She used to put two spoonfuls of sugar in the milk but had slowly weaned me down to half a spoonful and eventually to none at all.

"You don't want to end up looking like me," she'd said.

I'd been reasonably trim until the day she died. I now had the body type to qualify for this job.

"What would you tell an African-American child who said, 'I want to see the black Santa'?"

I realized I hadn't prepared at all for this interview, but I wasn't sure that or anything else mattered much anymore. Still, better to have a job take my mind away from Elaine than sit at home all day and brood. An admittedly somewhat rundown 1940's Tudor home with peeling trim that Elaine had already been asking me to renovate. Now I kept seeing our out-of-date kitchen through Elaine's eyes. I missed seeing it through Janice's.

So many happy Christmas dinners.

I'd been willing to look ahead, but now there seemed nothing worth anticipating.

"I'd say, 'I can be any color and look like anyone I want to, but right now I need to look like this.'"

Amanda smiled and wrote something down. "We actually do have black and Asian and sign language Santas, and we try to schedule people with the Santa they prefer, but you always get some who want a different Santa." She giggled. "No matter what you offer, people always want something more."

Elaine had wanted to go to Hawaii for our honeymoon. She'd only agreed on a ferry to Victoria if I would commit to Paris for our one-year anniversary.

"What would you tell a kid who said, 'I don't believe you're the *real* Santa'?"

I sighed. People were drinking coffee all around me. I'd never been inside a Starbucks before. I wondered if I should try a latte before I left. I'd heard that word often enough from coworkers. What did obeying the Word of Wisdom matter at this point? What did anything matter? If rules were important, I was never going to be with Janice in the next world in any event.

"I'd say something like, 'You don't have to believe for me to be here.'" I didn't want to lie. Lead people on.

"Good. Good," said Amanda. "That's actually one of our prompts."

"How many days a week would I be working?" I interrupted. "How long are the shifts?"

"Oh, it would be anywhere from one to four days, depending on need. And the shifts are anywhere from four to five hours. Believe me, that's a long time. Those suits are hot." She giggled again.

"And what's the pay?"

"$15.95 an hour."

I nodded. Enough to have taken Elaine to a nice restaurant at the end of the week.

I heard she was asking the Relief Society president to set her up with the president's widowed brother. He was almost seventy, with a nice pension from Boeing.

"So Barry," Amanda said, "what would you tell a kid who says, 'I don't believe Santa is real'?"

I looked at the half-empty cup of milk in front of me, looked out the window at people rushing down the street to shop, and then turned to Amanda. "I'd say, 'Yeah, and there's no God, either, you little fucker.'"

Amanda dropped her pen and stared. I stood up and walked out the door.

I walked from Westlake all the way to Pioneer Square, where I sat on a stone bench and watched a couple dozen homeless folks meandering about aimlessly. A woman ate something out of a paper bag. A man near her drank something out of another bag. Two other men sat together on the ground sharing a cigarette, even though the grass had to be cold and wet. It had rained yesterday.

"Why?" I said out loud, looking up into the sky. "Why?"

A heavyset woman in filthy clothes shuffled over and sat on the bench next to me. She thrust a half-eaten banana in my direction. I took the banana gingerly and looked at it for a long moment. Then I raised it to my lips and took a bite. The woman nodded at me and I nodded back. She shuffled on across the wet grass, leaving a trail like a slug. I watched while she nonchalantly swerved to avoid a man gesticulating into the air as if he were arguing with somebody, and I finished the banana in silence.

When I stepped off the 106 in Rainier Beach later, I walked straight to my house, pausing only a moment to look at the dark gray water of Lake Washington, with the hills of Mercer Island rising up in the middle. Where the rich people lived.

I had my memories of Janice, didn't I?

I went to the computer, picked up the phone, and hired two buses. Then I called the Relief Society president with the retired brother and had her activate her telephone tree to cancel invitations. The next evening, I wore an old pair of jeans and the pumpkin T-shirt when I welcomed 115 folks from the homeless shelter to my wedding banquet. I was skipping the meal myself, letting Marie Osmond persuade me to try Nutrisystem for a bit. Carolyn, her two sons, and their girlfriends were the only other official guests.

But I think my wife was there, too.

The Boycott

Ann put down her copy of *Lysistrata* and looked at the portrait of the First Presidency hanging on the living room wall. Her eyes narrowed as she scanned the other paintings in the room. Jesus Christ and Heavenly Father talking to Joseph Smith. Peter, James, and John ordaining Joseph. Brigham Young in his wagon entering the Salt Lake valley.

Ann frowned.

She'd heard through the grapevine that the radical group Ordain Women was going to try to gain admittance to the Priesthood session of General Conference in two weeks. Ann wasn't sure even Philip would be able to attend. It was a big conference center, but there were always thousands of men vying to get in from all around the world.

Ann had talked to Philip about her feelings many, many times. Philip's response was always, "You don't *need* the priesthood. You have *me*."

It had been difficult to raise her right hand to sustain Philip when he was called as bishop fourteen months ago. But she'd been a dutiful wife and done so. She'd believed that once in a position of substance, her husband would have more influence on the larger church and be able to help enlighten people to ideas of equality.

Unfortunately, since he didn't hold those ideas himself, he was hardly the right subject to proselytize them. Still, Ann was determined to at least get Philip to say something in Sacrament meeting just once about the Church needing to reevaluate its position on women and the priesthood.

And he needed to say something *before* General Conference. She would need to do something that left him no choice. He was already stressed to the max with both work and his clerical duties. It shouldn't take much to push him over the edge. She stared at the First Presidency and thought.

An hour later, Philip walked through the door. "Hi, honey, I'm home."

Ann walked up to meet him and kissed him gently on the lips. "How was your day, dear?"

"Tough. My boss is killing me." He took off his coat and hung it up.

"I'm so sorry."

"But I'll be boss one day soon myself."

"You're certainly cut out for it," said Ann. "I'm sorry you have to put up with him."

"Her."

"Oh, that's right."

"Well, it's nothing a plate of macaroni and cheese won't cure." Philip's eyes twinkled.

"Macaroni and cheese?" asked Ann innocently.

"It's Tuesday night, isn't it?"

"Oh, that." Ann smiled coyly. "Well, I decided that until you say in Sacrament meeting you think women ought to be ordained to the priesthood, I'm not cooking anymore."

"What?"

"No more dinners. No more breakfasts. No more preparing your lunch to take to work."

Philip laughed nervously. "That's not even funny, Ann."

"It sure isn't."

Philip's brows furrowed. "Ann, I've had a hard day. I'm the breadwinner around here. I pay all the bills. It's your job to be a wife and do the cooking and housework. If I do my share, you have to do yours."

"I'd be happy to," Ann said. "Once you make the announcement."

"I'm not being excommunicated just to fulfill some stupid whim. The Church will never ordain women to the priesthood. It wasn't done in the New Testament, and it wasn't done in the Book of Mormon. It simply isn't God's will."

"If I recall," Ann said brightly, "there was no Relief Society for women in the New Testament or Book of Mormon, either. No Primary, for that matter. No Institute." She batted her eyes innocently.

Philip stormed up the stairs and slammed the bedroom door. The kids, Ben and Susan, ten and eight, had just come down the stairs when their father pushed past them. They looked at Ann questioningly.

"How about chicken nuggets for dinner?" she said with a smile.

She obviously had to feed the kids, but it would be the simplest meals possible, no matter their nutritional value. They'd remember the boycott with fondness, regardless of Philip's actions.

Philip came downstairs just as the family was finishing up. He made no attempt to open the fridge or the pantry. He simply grabbed his coat and said, "I'm going out to eat." He opened the front door. "At that restaurant on Olive you like so much." Then he was out the door.

Ann laughed.

She was in bed when she heard the car pull back up in the driveway. Philip would have had to spend most of his evening at the church meeting with members. Members with problems. Members who would add to his stress. He came up the stairs, opened the bedroom door, and loudly clicked the light on, adjusting the dimmer so that the light shone at its brightest. He didn't say a word but noisily undressed, stomping about and slamming drawers.

Ann pretended to sleep through it all.

Philip plopped into bed roughly, trying to shake the mattress as much as possible. Ann continued to pretend to sleep. Philip kicked her in the leg, trying to pretend that was an accident.

Don't laugh, don't laugh, don't laugh, Ann told herself.

The next morning, Ann poured cereal for the kids and sent them off to school. She was eating a bagel with cream cheese when Philip showed up in the kitchen. He poured himself some orange juice and left without saying a word. Ann was sure he'd get tired of providing his own food long before she had her fill of his spitefulness.

She'd grown used to it over the years and built up a defense, since this was hardly his first display. Once, maybe two years ago, Ann had announced at the dinner table she'd applied for a part-time job at the library. Philip's immediate response was to say calmly, "If you interview for that position, I'll sell the second car."

Another time, she'd mentioned she was tired of doing genealogy at the Family History Library every Friday morning. "All the work will be done in the Millennium anyway," she'd said.

"No Family History," Philip had countered, "and no more gift cards from Barnes and Noble for you to waste all your time reading books." She'd given in that time, too. She had almost a thousand books. Philip always complained they were taking up too much space. And it wasn't as if she couldn't borrow from the library. But owning a book sometimes felt like the only freedom she had.

Ann spent the day reading another Greek play.

Around 5:15, the front door opened. "Honey, I'm home." Philip sounded cheerful. Ann's heart skipped a beat. Had he decided to give in so soon?

"Hi, sweetie," Ann gushed, running up and giving him a kiss. "How was your day?"

"Oh, just fine," he said with a grin. "During lunch, I went to the bank and took your name off the account. It's not joint anymore. No more money for you until you decide to act like a wife." He smiled and sauntered into the kitchen. "What's for dinner?"

"I had dinner already," Ann said sweetly. She'd known not to let her guard down. "A fried egg sandwich on toast. It really hit the spot. I know how much you like them, too."

Philip eyed her warily.

"I fed the kids early, too. They're upstairs doing their homework. Little angels." Ann had some money hidden in the house if she needed it. And Philip's new tactic simply meant *he'd* have to do the shopping and cooking for the kids himself once they ran out of what was already in the house. She could live with that.

"I want dinner," Philip said flatly.

"Be my guest." Ann started out of the kitchen. "Oh, I suppose I should mention, you only have one more clean shirt. And since I'm no longer doing your laundry, you might want to address that after you cook something for yourself." There actually had been several clean shirts still in his closet, but Ann had deliberately wrinkled six of them and tossed them in the hamper this morning.

"Well, I'm not taking out the garbage anymore."

"I'll get over it."

"And I'm taking back the keys of the car I let you use."

"You mean, my car?" Ann played along.

"No, *my* car. Everything here is mine. I paid for everything."

"All right, dear. Since I'm not buying groceries or running errands for you all day anymore, I suppose that's fair." She started to walk away but then turned back. "I think there are some saltines in the pantry."

"There are no ordained women in the Bible or Book of Mormon!"

Ann put her finger on her chin as if contemplating. "There are no sister missionaries, either, are there? Or Visiting Teachers? Or Home Teachers? Hmm, that *is* odd."

Ann walked up the stairs and closed the bedroom door. This had better work, she thought, or they were headed for a divorce. Why did men have to be such buttheads? She wondered for a moment if she were doing the right thing. She didn't particularly mind being a stay-at-home mom. She honestly did think it best for one parent to be available for the children. She just didn't think it always had to be the mother.

There was no reason a man couldn't stay at home and let his wife lead an exciting career. For that matter, there was no reason they couldn't both have part-time jobs and share the responsibility of raising the kids. There was no reason she *had* to be totally, one hundred percent dependent on her husband for everything.

Ann picked up the phone and called Betty, the wife of Philip's first counselor in the bishopric. She explained what she'd been doing and why, and Betty immediately asked, "Is it working?"

"It's too soon to tell," Ann replied, "but it'll work better if you do it, too. *Someone* in the bishopric will crack."

"Are you going to call Samantha?" The second counselor's wife.

"As soon as I hang up with you."

"All right," Betty said, "I'll give it a try. But only till Sunday."

Ann wasn't sure she'd have success that soon, but any help was useful. She dialed Samantha next and told her what both she and Betty were up to. "Grady is such a prick sometimes," Samantha told her. "Thinks his dick makes him a god. I'm with you."

"If we can keep this up for a couple of weeks," Ann said, "I'll call the stake president's wife."

"Well, she's in our ward, too. There's no reason she can't be in on this."

"She's a bit fanatical in her religious devotion," Ann mused, "but I did hear her in the bathroom at church a few weeks ago say something about how she could run the stake better than Fred."

Samantha laughed. "Call me tomorrow and we'll compare notes."

Ann read until 9:30 and then turned off the light. Perhaps half an hour later, Philip came in after another evening at church, surely exhausted and stressed again. He turned the light on as bright as it would go and stomped about as he had the night before. Then he turned the light down low.

Climbing into bed, he shook Ann's shoulder. "I want to make love," he declared.

This was the moment Ann had been waiting for. She'd heard about Ukrainian women vowing not to have sex with Russian men after the takeover of Crimea. She'd read about the women in Kenya, Liberia, and Colombia having their sex strikes to force men to their will. Sometimes it worked and sometimes it didn't. She thought again of *Lysistrata.*

"Oh, honey, I'm so anxious to make love to you, too." She watched him smile and said, "And we can do that just as soon as you take a stand publicly in church that women should be ordained to the priesthood."

Philip's face grew cold. "I can divorce you, you know."

"But they won't let you be bishop any longer."

"They won't let me be bishop if I say what you want me to say."

"But you'll still have me and the kids. An eternal family."

"Honey, you have to accept the facts. God didn't ordain women in the Bible and the Book of Mormon because he didn't want them to be ordained."

"I suppose that's possible, dear," Ann said slowly, "but I can't help but recognize there was no church university in those scriptures, either. No Family Home Evening. No Word of Wisdom. No Singles wards." She paused. "Do you think it's just remotely conceivable God doesn't need us to do everything the exact way it was done two thousand years ago?"

Philip deflated in front of her eyes, and Ann almost felt sorry for him. "I'm so tired," he mumbled.

"I'm thirty-two years old," Ann returned, "and I've heard every day of my life I'm not equal to men. You've had two hard days and *you* think *you're* tired!"

Philip sighed heavily. "All right. All right. I'll say something in Sacrament meeting this Sunday. Satisfied?"

"I will be on Sunday."

"So can we forget about all this and go back to normal?'

"Not until after Sacrament meeting on Sunday," Ann said. And maybe not even then, she realized. She wasn't sure a one-time announcement was going to put any kind of noticeable pressure on the Church. Maybe she should keep this up and spread it by word of mouth from one bishopric to another to another. People had cousins and sisters and friends in other wards and stakes across the country.

She could get a real movement going. They needed change, not just "pressure." Perhaps no one should give in until then, even if it took a year.

People said it would be at least fifty more years before the Church started treating women equally. But if even twenty percent of the women stopped having sex with their men, it would sure happen a lot sooner.

"All right. It's just a few more days. I'll go beat off in the bathroom." Philip started to climb out of bed.

"While you're in there," Ann said to his back as he walked away, "think about your brothers and college roommates and former mission companions you'll call tomorrow. You can ask them to say something in Sacrament meeting, too. They can offer to give talks or something. Your calling all of them is part of the deal, too."

She watched Philip hunch over at the words, but he didn't turn around. "Okay, honey."

She could hardly hear him.

Then he went in the bathroom and closed the door. Was this what power felt like, Ann mused? No wonder men didn't want to share it.

But sharing good things always made those things better. How often did one look back on a completely solitary moment in life and reminisce? Ann would share. When she and Philip worked together in a future temple presidency or as joint mission presidents after they retired, they'd create memories to last an eternity.

They could even go Home Teaching together, changing what was now a dreaded chore into quality time as a couple.

In the meantime, she could hide the starch so Philip would have to head to the store for a new can. She'd hide the extra toilet paper. She'd forget to remind him that since she no longer had access to the checking account, it was up to him to pay the household bills. And the electric bill was due yesterday.

Ann pulled the blanket up closer to her chin, thinking of new ways to torment her husband, and smiled.

Giving Yourself Completely

"No, Matt." Aaron shook his head. "We can't get fresh mozzarella for dinner."

"But it's so good," Matt replied, holding the small plastic tub under Aaron's nose, though there was no way to smell the cheese through the plastic. "You need a treat after all the stress you've been under. You're always doing sweet things for me. Can't I do something for you?"

It wasn't really a gift from Matt if the money wasn't coming from Matt's wallet, though, was it? "Buying expensive food when I'm out of a job will do nothing to alleviate my stress," he replied. Aaron shook his head again, and Matt put the mozzarella back in the display.

He hated being a jerk about it, but being fired at the age of sixty-two had put him in what seemed increasingly likely to be a permanent bad mood. His savings had held out almost six months, through his sixty-third birthday last week. He'd had no choice then but to start taking Social Security, but it only amounted to $1200 a month. Nowhere near enough to pay their monthly bills. Health insurance alone was outrageous.

"I'll think of *something* to make you feel better." Matt reached over to squeeze Aaron's behind. Aaron wasn't big on PDA's to begin with, and certainly not inappropriate ones. He swatted Matt's hand away.

Matt looked hurt and returned his gaze to the grocery list. Aaron stared at the younger man's blond hair, only just now starting to gray at the temples. Why the boy put up with the constant scolding, Aaron didn't know. He hated himself for it but just couldn't seem to stop.

Part of the problem was growing up black in Mississippi. Even after moving to Portland, where there was at least a meager attempt at equality, Aaron still felt inferior. He saw Michelle Obama and Condoleeza Rice and marveled at their self-assurance. He could never be like that. He felt ashamed if he spoke "white" in a conversation with other blacks. He felt ignorant when talking with whites. So often, he didn't know things everyone else seemed to have known by the age of eight.

He felt like an abomination for wanting sex with other men, made worse because he'd been a Mormon since the age of twelve. Not that his Baptist relatives tolerated it any better.

And he felt ugly—uglier and uglier every year—knowing he only had a "relationship" with Matt because he'd hired the boy seventeen years ago for a quick screw and was so infatuated he'd asked the hustler to move in two weeks later, though the young man had clearly felt no attraction in return.

Well, Matt wasn't a young man. He was almost forty now. But he'd never worked a regular job in his life. No one would hire him at this point with no resumé. At least that was what Matt kept saying whenever he submitted an application and never heard back. No one would hire Aaron, either. Because he was black. Because he was old. Because he couldn't keep up with computers.

Because Heavenly Father didn't love him.

No one loved him. Not even Matt. Matt just liked being taken care of. Aaron gave himself to Matt over and over and over, and while Matt was always pleasant enough, all he did was take. He took the gym membership. He took the wine club membership. He took the nice clothes.

Of course, all that was over now.

"How about some bananas?" asked Matt. "You like bananas, and they don't cost much."

Aaron nodded, and Matt put a bunch of seven almost-ripe bananas in the basket. Aaron suspected the white shoppers nearby were thinking about him eating like a monkey. But then, if he ever put paté or olives or some other fancy item in his basket, he was sure everyone was thinking he was trying to live too high.

The bishop wouldn't help Aaron with his bills because he was gay. Not even any food from the Bishop's Storehouse. Nothing. And he'd been going to church all his adult life, even after coming out. He even paid his tithing every month until he lost his job. He was trying to be a good man despite his carnal weaknesses.

Would he have managed to become a better person if he'd ever felt truly loved? Nicer? Stronger? He tried to imagine the greatness he might have had.

Well, that was all moot now.

"That's enough," Aaron said when Matt put a package of frozen spinach in the basket. "I'm sure we're at our budget."

"But there's so much left on the list."

"We'll eat rice and pasta."

Matt's lip curled and Aaron stared at him a long moment. How could the boy look so lovely even when he was mad? He was exquisite, everything you could want in a white man. He even had a decent-sized dick. And he was so good at fucking. Aaron loved to be fucked. He *deserved* to be fucked. It was nice enjoying something you deserved.

He wondered briefly if that was what Outer Darkness would be like after he died. Enjoying his punishment for eternity.

Would Satan fuck him personally? Or beat him? Maybe he'd love being beaten.

They stood in the checkout line, and Aaron watched the cashier's face as her eyes lingered on him for a second, then on Matt, then on Aaron again. It was the same whether the cashier was white or black. Asians didn't seem to notice or care. It was bad enough having everyone know he was gay, but he knew everyone was also wondering why an ugly old black man was with a young, beautiful white man. They had to know he was paying Matt to stay with him. He could see it in their eyes.

No one else had ever wanted to be with him. He'd been forty-five before he finally gave up loneliness and asked Matt to move in. Aaron hadn't really minded paying all the bills.

He had a decent job. And Matt had done literally everything Aaron ever asked him to do. He cleaned the house. He cooked. And he kept Aaron happy in bed.

But it would be two more years before Aaron qualified for Medicare. He needed his blood pressure medication. He needed his cholesterol meds.

He wasn't going to make it two more years without any money.

Matt drove them home and helped put the groceries away. As he closed the last cabinet, Matt gave Aaron a grim smile. His eyes narrowed and then he pushed Aaron over the kitchen table.

"Umphh! What are you doing?"

"Shut up and take it." Matt pulled Aaron's pants down around his knees, grabbed a bottle of olive oil for lube, and pushed his way inside him. Aaron wished he'd used the canola oil. It was cheaper. Matt fucked him hard. It almost felt as if the boy had torn him. But it also felt so, so good.

Maybe the best thing would be for Matt to fuck him to death. Then he wouldn't have to worry about anything at all anymore.

Matt zipped up. They kissed. And then Matt started preparing dinner.

There was little talk during the meal, and afterward, Matt turned on the stereo so they could cuddle on the sofa without saying a word. Matt had put in a Natalie Cole CD. Aaron loved her, but he could never get that awful *Saturday Night Live* commercial out of his head. "*Unforgiveable*. The new

CD out now at your local store! Listen to Natalie Cole sing with her dad's dead friends!"

What Aaron had done was unforgiveable.

Even though he knew Matt only saw him as a meal ticket, he so wished they could be together for eternity. Would they be able to get sealed during the Millennium? Would the Church ever seal a man and his prostitute? He wanted to be Richard Gere and have Matt be Julia Roberts as they rode off into the sunset together.

Matt rested his head on Aaron's stomach, and Aaron caressed his hair gently. Matt had become more distant lately, had disappeared for hours at a time and refused to explain where he'd been. Not that Aaron normally checked up on him. He understood that someone so beautiful needed to find outside attractions. He expected the boy was looking for another Daddy. It was clear Aaron could no longer take care of him, but he couldn't bear the thought of being abandoned by someone he was paying.

"What are we going to do, honey?" Aaron asked softly. "I don't know what we're going to do."

"I'll find a job," said Matt. "Even if it's just cashiering. Somebody will hire me sooner or later if I just keep applying."

Aaron knew Matt wasn't applying anymore, that he didn't want to be "common." He wouldn't even trick on the side these days for a little extra cash. That kind of thing was beneath him now. He'd turned to donating sperm and plasma every few days, but one couldn't make a living on that.

"We just need enough for you to pay your insurance premiums. And only for two years. We can do that."

Aaron thought about the $18,000 he still owed on the house, the $2000 left on the car. He thought about the other monthly bills. The mozzarella they both enjoyed. The expensive underwear Matt looked so sexy in.

"You've been so good to me," Matt whispered. "So good. Always giving yourself completely. I'll—"

It sounded like the boy was getting ready to leave him. Aaron closed his eyes. He knew that if he was being honest, he'd never given himself *completely* to Matt. What would have been the point? He always understood that their abominable relationship had no future. And now he was going to come home from job hunting one day, the closet emptied. After all the years he'd devoted to Matt. Even 70% devotion over seventeen years still amounted to something, didn't it?

Aaron couldn't help but think how things might have been if gay love were equal to straight. What might he have achieved if he'd ever felt truly loved even once in his life?

What would such an incredible feeling feel like?

Matt sat up and Aaron tensed. "Aaron…?"

"Yes?"

"Will you fuck me?"

Aaron's mouth fell open. He'd never fucked Matt before. The boy had asked for it, but Aaron only felt right being fucked himself. He wasn't sure he could do it. "Why?"

"I just want you to fuck me." He looked steadily into Aaron's eyes. "Please?"

Aaron nodded and led Matt to the bedroom. He had his Vaseline Intensive Rescue lotion which always felt good inside his own ass, so he slathered some on his penis and inserted it gently into Matt's backside. Aaron was surprised the sensation felt so good. It really did. It felt *good.*

All these years they might have been taking turns.

Well, maybe it wasn't too late.

"Thanks, punkin," Matt said when Aaron had finished. "Thank you."

Aaron wanted to cry.

"We'll get through this," Matt promised. "Please don't worry. We'll get through this."

Aaron had a glass of warm milk and then climbed into bed. Matt said he wanted to stay up a little longer, maybe look online for more jobs. They kissed, and Aaron listened to his bedside CD player. Waves crashing on shore. Wouldn't it be great if he and Matt lived in a lighthouse in Maine?

Aaron drifted off to sleep, dreaming of rocky beaches, snug inside beside a fireplace. He awoke around 3:00 to go pee, unnerved to see that Matt hadn't come to bed yet. After finishing in the bathroom, he headed for the living room. No Matt. He checked the office. No Matt there, either.

But there was a letter.

Dearest love of my life,

I know I've never been much good, but now I can do something real for you, finally, something that matters. I've talked to someone. Did you know people will buy eyes for $1500? That they'll buy a skull with teeth for $1000? Did you know a heart can go for as much as $110,000 and a liver for $150,000? Kidneys go for about $200,000 each. People will even buy skin at $10 a square inch.

Anyway, you understand. No one will ever find any part of me. It's all being sold. I've arranged for you to get 20%. That should come to about $130,000. Enough to get you through the next few years.

I will miss you. But I know we'll be together again. I'll wait patiently for you.

Love always,

Matt

Aaron stood over the desk, stunned. Then he noticed that Matt had printed out an online coupon. It was for fresh mozzarella.

Aaron collapsed into the chair and stared at the letter for a long while. He felt as if he'd been punched in the chest. He rubbed his sternum absentmindedly a few moments and then stumbled back to bed. He didn't call the police. He half-expected Matt to spring through the doorway and announce he was just joking. But another part of him recognized it was true.

Aaron knew he might be damned to hell for not going to the bishop, but he was simply too happy to allow himself to call. Someone loved him! He felt whiter than he'd ever felt. And blacker. He felt taller.

Maybe they *could* get married after the Resurrection.

In the morning, Aaron listened to Etta James singing "At Last." He wouldn't leave the house, in case someone came to contact him about Matt. He sat at the kitchen table, rationing his food, fingering the coupon Matt had left. If no money ever came, he'd finally have to report the crime, but surely, Matt's contact knew that, too. The money would come.

He went through the remainder of the supplies in eight days, but he still wouldn't leave the house. He wouldn't take any calls unless it was a number he didn't recognize. Maybe it would be "them." Finally, on the ninth day, around 11:30 at night, there was a knock on the door. Aaron ran to answer it.

There was a briefcase on the doormat. Aaron picked it up, looking around, but saw no one. He brought the case inside, set it on the kitchen table, and opened it. There were stacks of hundred dollar bills. Aaron breathed in relief. It was all true. He counted the money quickly. Twenty thousand dollars. And a note. "Payment in full."

Aaron collapsed into one of the kitchen chairs. "Oh, Matt."

He stared at the stacks of bills in front of him. He reached over to pull out a single hundred dollar note. Then he picked up the coupon for mozzarella, already fraying from all the times he'd toyed with it. He stood up slowly and sighed. Then he went outside and climbed wearily into the car. He turned on a CD of Gladys Knight and headed for hustler row.

Burying My Baby at Deseret Land and Livestock

The last time my stake hosted a Mormon Handcart reenactment, I was fourteen and just getting over a sprained ankle from gymnastics class, so I hadn't participated. Now I was seventeen, old for a Laurel, soon to become a much anticipated Single Adult. I still wasn't sure the Trek sounded all that exciting, but the bishop, stake president, and Laurel president were all pushing the three-day adventure quite hard.

"You'll get to experience what our ancestors did," my mom pointed out again this evening over dinner.

"The Jews don't celebrate their slavery in Egypt by becoming slaves for three days," I said. "They have a great meal while reclining."

"You can't have empathy unless you truly understand what our forefathers and mothers went through," Dad said.

"Do I need to be tarred and feathered to appreciate Joseph Smith?"

"Now, Melanie, be nice."

I finished my dinner and went upstairs. I didn't even have chores like dishwashing, I realized, lying on my bed. Maybe I truly was a bit spoiled living in the 21st century.

Perhaps three days pushing a handcart in northern Utah wouldn't be overly detrimental to my emotional health. Still, we wouldn't be allowed to bring our cell phones, so there'd be no texting for three days. What were we, Neanderthals?

I'd already had to sew a period dress I'd be wearing. But at least they'd let us bring our tennis shoes. I called my best friend, Jen.

"What do you think?" I asked. "Are you going?"

"My parents said I'd be grounded for three whole weeks if I didn't."

"I love the subtle way gospel principles are taught." I laughed but Jen did not.

"Three days spending the night in sleeping bags with ticks everywhere?" she asked. "Three days of porta-potties?"

"Just look at it as training for BYU," I said.

"What do you mean?" Both Jen and I planned to go to Brigham Young University next year.

"They have a Study Abroad course where you get to walk the entire 1400 mile trek the pioneers used on the Mormon Trail."

"Oh, my heck. Don't tell my parents that!"

We talked about the cute non-member boy named David who sometimes attended Sunday school, and about mean Brother Sidney who taught the class. We made fun of Sister Patterson, the teacher for the MIA Maids, for a few minutes and then hung up.

My parents were making me pay the $15 participation fee for the Trek out of my allowance. Talk about suffering for my faith.

On Thursday morning, Mom dropped me off at church, and I sat next to Jen as our Laurel president drove us and a couple of younger girls to Woodruff. There were about fifteen to twenty kids from each ward, and nine wards in the stake, so there'd be about 180 teens participating, plus a few adult chaperones. I'd be wearing this same yellow dress for three days, but I had a small pack with extra underwear and socks. And a few Almond Joy bars I'd smuggled with me.

Jen leaned over and whispered, "I've got six granola bars if you ever get desperate out there, Melanie."

Granola sounded too much like what the pioneers might have eaten.

We arrived at Deseret Land and Livestock still early in the morning, a huge Church farm that promised twenty-five miles of ranch roads and cross-country walking. "All right," a man said after everybody was out of the cars and vans and standing in a huge crowd, "this is Brother and Sister Clawson. They're a missionary couple and will go with you on the Trek. They'll be able to tell you pioneer stories at night after dinner. And here are Tom Bradley and Derek Peters. They're two recreation students. They'll be assisting you along the way."

Jen nudged me and nodded toward Derek.

"We'll be providing a water trailer and the porta-john trailer, and of course the handcarts, but your stake leaders will provide the food. You'll have essentials with you on the

Trek, but someone will drive to appointed meeting places and bring the suppers." He smiled broadly. "So you see, it won't be as bad as some of you imagined."

"Where's the trailer carrying the Xboxes?" shouted a boy in back of the crowd. Everyone laughed.

"You'll find it a relief to be away from modern civilization a few days," the man assured us. "In fact, you may find you want to turn off the computer when you get back home. Many of—"

"What if I get a blister?" shouted another boy. More laughter.

"We have Sister Gunderson with us," announced a man from one of the other wards. "She's a registered nurse."

The introductory pep talk continued a few more minutes. We'd be at an elevation between 6500 and 7500 feet for the next three days. The area consisted of rolling hills covered in prairie grass and sage, with some small canyons here and there. As residents of Utah, we already knew how to watch out for snakes and scorpions. "Or should I say, as residents of Zion?" There were a few weak chuckles.

I looked out beyond the tiny headquarters. The area looked bleak and barren, not a tree in sight. But then, as a "resident of Zion," I was already used to that. We were divided into teams to push handcarts filled with our sleeping bags and backpacks, some food, and a little water that would be available in addition to the water trailer. Of course, I chose to walk with Jen. There were also two boys from another ward, and two girls from yet another. I was glancing at my watch, which I wasn't supposed to be wearing, when Sister

Clawson, the missionary lady, came up to me with a baby doll. She thrust it at me.

"What's this?" I asked.

"Several of the older girls are being chosen to become mothers," Sister Clawson replied. "Many of the women who crossed the plains had to carry babies in addition to pushing the handcarts."

My mouth fell open. I took the doll and tried to hold it while testing whether or not I'd still be able to push. This was going to be a pain in the butt.

Sister Clawson smiled and moved along to find her next "mother."

"Oh, maybe this'll be fun, after all," Jen said, eyeing my baby jealously.

"If I'm married," I replied, "do I get to have sex around the campfire with my husband tonight?"

Jen giggled. "You're so bad." One of the boys assigned to our cart winked at me. I'd seen him a time or two at stake events and thought he was cute, but I wasn't sure he was all that active, because there were lots of activities he should have been present at but wasn't. Maybe the Trek was his way of becoming more faithful.

Soon we were off, singing "for some must push and some must pull" as we went. It was already hot. As it turned out, while I tried to hold my baby with one arm and push with the other, this was just too awkward, and most of the time, I just walked. One of the girls from the other ward who were with our handcart said loudly to the other, "Why does *she* get the baby?"

The other girl replied, just as loudly, "Because she looks so matronly." Then both girls sniggered.

That was offset slightly during one of our breaks, when the boy who'd winked at me earlier came in back and said, "I'd let you carry *my* baby anytime." He'd been looking over his shoulder at me and making cute comments the whole trip. After his latest remark, he casually scratched at his crotch and grinned.

"Well, I never!" said the girl who'd called me matronly.

"At this rate, you never will," the boy informed her. Then he offered his hand to me. "Roger," he said.

"Melanie."

He leaned over and whispered. "Tonight after everyone's asleep, I'll come over to your sleeping bag."

"How will you find me in the dark?"

"They'll keep a few lights on so we can find our way to the bathrooms."

I nodded. "And what will you do once you find me?"

"We'll just kiss tonight," he whispered. "It's only our first date." He paused and glanced over at the girl looking haughtily at us. "But on the *third* night…" His voice trailed away, and I smiled. Of course I would never do anything more than kiss on a date in any event, but it was fun to feel bold and decadent. Even the chaperones had to sleep at some point. This trek might be more fun than I'd thought.

We continued on our walk, very slowly, between one and two miles an hour. That was almost worse than walking at a normal pace, but with the handcarts, it was difficult to go any faster. I noticed one girl from the handcart in front of us had to make frequent trips to the porta-john wagon. I wondered if she was menstruating. How awful and embarrassing. Thank God it wasn't my time of the month. How miserable *that* must have been in the old days. And as disgusting as the porta-johns themselves were, I was grateful we weren't expected to use the alternative the pioneers had.

We stopped again for lunch, and while I wasn't exhausted, I realized I'd be pretty tired by the end of the day. Walking all day every day for three solid months truly must have been quite the ordeal, I thought.

"Hey, my clothes are all dirty," said a boy from one of the other handcarts. "I fell down back there."

"Well, you'll just have to stay dirty for the next three days," said one of the adults near him. "There were certainly no washers and dryers back in the day."

The rest of the afternoon plodded along uneventfully. Earlier in the morning, we'd sung lots of pioneer songs and hymns. Now everyone was too tired. Even just standing in this heat hours would have been exhausting, much less walking while pushing or pulling a handcart. Or carrying a baby. I began to realize I was one of the lucky ones. A doll wasn't as heavy as that handcart.

"Wanna trade?" asked Jen, eyeing my baby enviously. "Mothers back in pioneer days probably traded."

Jen looked tired, so I agreed. She took the baby with a smile, and I assumed her place pushing the cart. Sure enough, it wasn't as fun as the bishop had made it sound during his encouraging talk a couple of weeks ago. I took the baby back around 5:00, and though there was still plenty of light left, the commander of the group, a man from another ward, soon called a halt for the day. There was a soft cheer.

Before long, a couple of minivans showed up, and the leaders organized the kids to start cooking. It turned out that two of the handcarts were carrying barbecues. "We don't want to start a wildfire," one of the men explained.

The boys ended up doing most of the cooking, hamburgers and roasted potatoes. It was strange having potatoes in place of French fries, but satisfying enough. I thought it odd that indoors, women were always expected to be in the kitchen, but being outdoors suddenly made cooking masculine, and the boys fought over the grill.

"No pickle relish?" asked a boy, looking forlornly at his dry hamburger. "Those pioneers really did rough it."

I had to hold the baby in my lap while I ate, and Jen kept giggling every time I let the doll slide down. Once I found myself resting my elbows on it. Even Roger laughed. "I see why so many infants died along the trail," he said. I stuck out my tongue at him.

"I want to see more of that tongue later," he said.

The girl who'd called me matronly glared at us. I simply said, "There won't be *that* many lights. You'll have to feel your way around."

"I'm up for feeling my way." He made a motion as if squeezing a melon in the air. I instinctively put my arm across my chest.

After supper was over and everything had been cleaned up, it was still light, though getting late. Everyone gathered around the elderly missionary couple who'd apparently brought lawn chairs along on one of the handcarts. The rest of us were sitting on the ground. "Time for pioneer stories," Brother Clawson announced.

"I know some of you have sore feet," he said, "but did you know there were many pioneers, especially children and teenagers whose feet kept growing too fast for their parents to keep buying them new shoes, who actually walked the entire way barefoot?"

There was a low gasp from the crowd. "Many arrived in the Salt Lake Valley with their feet all bloodied. That's how much they cared about getting to the Promised Land."

I looked about at the dreary landscape.

"And there were lots of young people your age who were real heroes on some of these treks," Brother Clawson went on. "You've probably heard of the Martin handcart company, who were so anxious to get to Salt Lake they started out too late in the season rather than wait a whole year. Unfortunately, the snows came early, and they suffered terribly and were finally stranded. When Brigham Young heard about their plight, he sent a rescue party, which reached the group at Sweetwater River in Wyoming.

"The group had to cross that big, icy river, and most of them simply weren't up to it. So three teenage boys, boys your age, carried almost every single member of the Martin party across that river by hand. They saved dozens of lives." He paused dramatically. "But all three boys died later of complications they suffered for their heroism." There was silence among the group. "That's what being a hero means, doing the right thing regardless of the consequences." He looked out at all of us. "Do *you* always do the right thing?"

The stories continued for another forty minutes, until it really did grow dark. I'd been expecting a campfire at some point. Camping always seemed to revolve around campfires, so I was surprised when the leaders brought out several battery-charged lanterns and set them up at strategic intervals. The boys were directed to lay out their sleeping bags on one side of the line of handcarts, and the girls were directed to the opposite side.

"Time for snakes to slide in with us to stay warm," Jen muttered.

I rarely went to bed this early, but I had to admit, I was quite tired, and I still had two more days of this crap to go through. Jen and I chatted in our bags for a few minutes, but then I could tell she'd fallen asleep, and I wasn't far behind. While I'd been out of gymnastics for over a year, I dreamed about doing hours of drills.

Sometime later, I felt someone nudging me. "Huh?" I mumbled.

"Shh! It's me, Roger."

I awoke almost immediately, astonished he'd actually come over. To my surprise, he didn't sit or lie down beside me but lay directly on top of my sleeping bag. "What do you think you're doing?" I hissed.

"It's perfectly safe," Roger whispered back. "We have this barrier between us. It'll be okay." And with that, he put his lips against mine and kissed me. Although I'd been dating boys for a year, I'd never kissed before. Most boys only took me on one date, so there was never any time to work up to greater intimacy. I knew Mom didn't want me kissing at all, saying I should wait to kiss for my first time over the altar in the temple, but I'd been wondering about it for ages and couldn't resist when the opportunity was thrust upon me.

"Shh," Roger whispered a few minutes later. "You're moaning."

There was a fumbling attempt at groping through the sleeping bag, but the material was too thick to allow much satisfaction. Still, kissing alone was enough. Roger lay on top of me for a full thirty minutes. Finally, he pulled back and whispered, "That was Date Number One. Just wait till tomorrow night."

I was glad Mom had insisted I come on this trip.

Roger crept off again to his side of the handcarts, and while I tried to think about kissing, I was soon back asleep.

In the morning, I was dying to tell Jen what had happened, but there just wasn't enough privacy. After a quick breakfast of bacon and eggs, we all gathered our belongings back onto the handcarts and took off again. It felt odd not having a real goal. The pioneers could feel every day they were just that much closer to Salt Lake, but we were merely wandering about the Deseret Land and Livestock farm simply to be wandering. I felt more like a Jew following Moses in the desert for forty years than a Mormon pioneer.

We sang pioneer songs and hymns again, Jen and I trading off carrying the baby. It got to be where I started to hate the damn thing. Even pushing the cart felt more useful than carrying a piece of plastic. At least this wasn't one of those new fancy dolls that "messed" its diaper. I was sure the leaders had considered it, just to make the trek more miserable, but whatever their reasons were for deciding against it, I was grateful.

"Hey," said Roger during a break. "Why don't you come pull the cart with me for a bit while Tim here goes in back and helps push?"

We tried that arrangement, and Roger and I were able to talk for about ten minutes, but it soon became apparent I was a pusher, not a puller, so Tim and I switched places again. "Using a spiritual Church outing to flirt with a boy," muttered the girl who'd called me matronly. I still hadn't asked her name. "No wonder you ended up with a baby."

Jen and I talked about Sunday school for a while, how we almost fell asleep last week until Brother Sidney slapped the table with his Book of Mormon. We talked about Sister Patterson, who was clearly after Brother Sidney, for some unfathomable reason. And then Jen said, "Can I have David now that you have Roger?"

"He's still a non-member," I pointed out.

"I can fix that. He comes to church, doesn't he?"

"Sometimes."

Soon we stopped for lunch, and then we were walking again. In some ways, today was easier than the day before because I was "in the groove." But in other ways, walking was becoming very tedious. I was athletic by nature and never minded a good hour-long walk once in a while. But this was hour after hour after hour after hour. My feet tingled the entire time we were on breaks.

And there was nothing to look at but short prairie grass as far as the eye could see. That and the back of the handcart in front of me. You could only chat with your best friend just so long before you ran out of things to say. Yesterday, there'd been a buzz about the group even when we weren't singing. Today, there were huge spans of silence, only the sounds of the creaking handcart wheels to fill the air.

We were so tired by dinner that even hot dogs and potato chips couldn't cheer us up. The minivans had brought ketchup this time, so supper was quite a treat. I was just too tired to appreciate it. "What you need is a *real* hot dog," Roger told me.

"Oh, brother," said the matronly girl in disgust.

We had another session of pioneer stories after supper. Sister Clawson spoke about pioneer girls this time. "Mary Iverson's mother was sick and was tired of drinking melted snow. She asked Mary, who was sixteen, to go find a stream and bring back fresh water. While they were stopped, Mary went to look for a stream, but she was so afraid of the Indians in the area who'd been following them that she got distracted and ended up lost.

"The snow was almost to her knees, and by the time she was found, she had frostbite. She never did find the stream to bring back fresh water for her mother, but by the time she got back to the camp, her mother had died anyway. Three of Mary's brothers and sisters had died in the previous weeks, but now she was left in charge of her one remaining baby brother. They were living on just one ounce of flour a day. When she arrived in Salt Lake, she had her toes amputated. She found a good man who married her and helped raise her brother and their own seven children. She lived a good, gospel-centered life because she crossed those plains and came to Salt Lake."

And I had slipped out to Starbucks two months ago to try my first latte, I thought. I should be ashamed of myself, when my ancestors had been through so much to provide me with the gospel.

The lanterns were set up and everyone in their sleeping bags even earlier than the night before. Jen was saying something to me about wanting to wash her hair when I fell into a deep sleep almost instantly. Sometime during the night, I was vaguely aware of someone touching me. I opened my eyes, but unlike the previous evening, tonight I was still groggy. Roger unzipped my sleeping bag and lay on top of me. His weight felt quite comfortable. I wanted nothing more than to sleep with him lying there. He tried kissing my lips, but I was rather unresponsive, I suppose, so he just kissed my cheeks and then my shoulders.

I did fall asleep again but then suddenly awakened when I felt something entering me. I gasped and was about to cry out when Roger put his lips over mine. We weren't supposed to be doing this, I wanted to say. It hurt a little, yet somehow also felt good. His weight and his kisses were sublime. And I felt like a real woman for the first time. I'd just decided to push him off anyway when he groaned and rolled over. He'd only been on top of me a couple of minutes.

"I told you the second date would be better," he whispered.

I wondered what our third date would be like the following evening. After Roger sneaked quietly back to his side of the handcarts, I looked up at the stars and wondered what to do. There was Taurus, I noticed, and Leo. But the stars couldn't distract me for long. I'd just had sex, when two days ago I'd never even kissed a boy. What was I going to do? Should I tell my bishop when I got home? Should I tell my parents? Should I tell Jen?

Or should I keep my mouth shut? Just because I'd done it once didn't mean I had to do it again. I could still go to the temple. Maybe with Roger when he got back from his mission. I could wait for him.

I was up another twenty minutes reflecting, but then the fatigue of the day settled back in and I fell asleep once more.

In the morning after another round of bacon and eggs, I headed for the porta-john trailer. There were two adult men talking. They glanced in my direction, but since I was still exhausted, I must have looked oblivious. I didn't even realize what they were saying for the first few moments. Then I began to hear.

"I liked the old days better," one of the men said, "when we only had johnnie cake and molasses on these trips, and the trips lasted a whole week, not just three short days. And we pushed the kids to walk farther every day, and we really had the chance to break their spirits, just like a horse's. You could create a spiritual conversion back then once you broke someone's spirit. Now these kids'll go home thinking they're great, then go back to being the same rotten kids they were before."

"I'm not rotten," I wanted to say, but then I remembered last night. Maybe I *was* rotten. At the same time, what had happened *almost* seemed like a spiritual experience. Maybe Roger and I would take our time tonight and I'd learn what it felt like to truly experience love.

The pioneer songs and hymns lasted a little longer this morning, everyone psyched up despite their fatigue, knowing this was the last day. Jen and I ended up tying the baby to my back so I could help push along with her. We took two breaks before lunch, and then a long lunch break. "You seem to have a certain glow about you today," Roger said, smiling at me and winking.

I stuck out my tongue.

"I want to see more of that later."

The girl who'd called me matronly snorted.

I was just dying to talk openly with Jen, but I realized I might not be able to tell her even after we got home. She might say something to someone. As we trudged across the hills after lunch, I kept sneaking a look at my watch. Soon this would all be over. Soon I'd be home.

But even sooner would be tonight's date.

"I can't wait to take a bath," Jen said.

"Think our folks will expect us to go to church Sunday?" I asked.

"Oh, they'll expect it, but they're not going to get it." She laughed. "It's the least I can get out of this."

Around three in the afternoon, during one of our breaks, Brother Clawson came over while I was sipping water and flicking some in Roger's face. "Your baby has just died," he said calmly.

"What?"

"It happened often during these treks. Your baby died, and now you have to bury it." He handed me a spade. I took the tool and looked at him in confusion. "We used to make the girls dig the graves with sticks," he explained, "but we use spades now. Go dig a grave, and you can have this young man…" He pointed at Roger. "…say a blessing over it."

Brother Clawson kept walking through the crowd, picking out several other "mothers" who'd just lost their babies. I couldn't believe they'd calculated all this.

"I'm so sorry for your loss," Jen said. I couldn't tell if she was serious or joking.

"Come on," said Roger. "I'll help you dig."

We walked off about thirty yards from the main group and knelt in the prairie grass. Roger took the spade and began. "Gives us a chance to be alone," he said. He looked at me and smiled broadly. "I really like you, Melanie."

I smiled back. "I'm glad we're on the same team." I wanted to ask if he'd call me, but I didn't want to sound desperate.

It took us half an hour, but we finally buried the doll, and Roger even managed to offer a brief prayer, despite the fact none of this was real. I admired him for it. Maybe we had sinned once, but we'd be good from now on and get married in the temple after he came back from overseas.

We joined the others, who'd simply been grateful to have a longer than normal break, and we set off on our last segment of the journey. We met up with the minivans around 5:15 and had our last supper, pork and beans with potato salad and tiny sausages.

I wished I had a Coke.

There were no pioneer stories this evening. Tonight was saved for a testimony meeting. For a while, it seemed almost everyone in the entire party planned to bear their testimony. I thought the meeting would never end. There were tearful speeches about "finally understanding the sacrifices our forefathers made" and "feeling closer to Heavenly Father and Jesus Christ than ever before." The adults looked on, almost smirking rather than smiling.

But eventually, around 9:00, Brother Clawson offered a prayer, and we headed for our sleeping bags. As excited as I was to see Roger again, I was still completely exhausted and decided to take a nap before his visit. Like before, I awakened later to find him kneeling over me. I pulled him down and kissed him. He unzipped my bag, spread my legs, and entered me again. I wrapped my arms around his back and luxuriated thoroughly in the experience. When he finished several minutes later, I whispered, "Do it again."

Roger laughed softly. "I can only come twice, you know."

"Well, how many times have you come?" I laughed.

"I already did it with Sue once."

I stared at him in the darkness, hardly able to make out his face. "Who's Sue?"

"That girl who doesn't like you."

"You had sex with *her* this evening?" I said, astounded.

"Yes, but I picked you to be last because I knew the second time would take longer. I like you better."

I unwrapped my arms from around Roger's back.

"Can I call you next Saturday?" he whispered.

"After going out with Sue on Friday?" I whispered back.

He laughed. "What do you care what I do Friday, as long as I'm with you on Saturday?" He caressed my face. "We're here to learn to live like the pioneers. The pioneers practiced polygamy, you know."

"I think you better go back to your side of the camp."

"Wait a second," said Roger, and he did wait a few moments before speaking again, fondling himself. "I think I can come a third time." He put his hands between my legs.

I sighed and opened up, letting Roger inside again. A learning experience, I supposed. It took him fifteen minutes this time. I lay back and stared up at the stars, trying to find Scorpio as Roger pumped away, and looking forward to the long trip back to Salt Lake in the morning.

Only in Salt Lake

"I still don't understand why you insisted on coming to Salt Lake," said Cathy, peering at the spot on the conveyor belt where the luggage was emerging.

"Sally's dating a Mormon boy," Steve replied. "We may as well pretend to appreciate his culture."

"But I'm hoping they'll break up," Cathy pointed out.

"You keep sending her those links to articles about LDS history," Steve warned, "and you'll drive her right into his arms."

"Maybe I should be sending those links to him."

"Live and let live, okay? It's not as if we have a religion of our own."

"I suppose. But do you want our grandchildren working as missionaries in Kenya?"

"Why not? What better way to get an appreciation for the interconnection between all people? Maybe we can learn something."

Cathy ignored him, and Steve looked about at the suitcases rolling past. Cathy had never been one to explore the larger world culture, he reflected. She was content with the Walmart in Sioux City. She didn't even know anything about the Sioux. They'd only taken two vacations in the last ten years, one to Branson and one to Orlando. At least this time, Steve insisted on something a little less white bread.

Cathy stamped her foot. "Where's our luggage?"

New bags had stopped issuing out onto the conveyor belt ten minutes ago. Most of the other passengers had grabbed their luggage and left. "Maybe we're at the wrong carousel," Steve said.

"Didn't you recognize the other passengers?" countered Cathy. "This is the right place."

They waited patiently another fifteen minutes, talking about what they might eat for dinner, and what kind of view they hoped their hotel room offered. Steve was hoping to keep Cathy calm. They hadn't had sex in almost three weeks. He planned to try at least twice on this trip. Maybe they could jumpstart their sexual relationship altogether. Lately, it seemed all Cathy was interested in was shoes.

Not his, of course. Even a foot fetish would have been something to welcome. No, Cathy just liked shopping for new shoes of her own, regardless of how many she already possessed. They were mostly Walmart shoes, so it wasn't as if she was breaking the bank. But it was clear she was trying to make up for some other lack in her life, and Steve didn't want that lack to be him. He realized he hadn't been as attentive lately as he should've been. He was determined now to be more romantic and pay better attention to her, even if he had to fake a foot fetish himself. "Your toenails are pretty in those sandals," he said.

Cathy didn't seem to hear and approached an airport employee. "Where's our luggage?" she demanded.

The employee pointed to the carousel, which had one sole suitcase on the floor beside it. "Your luggage was on that flight?" he asked. When Cathy nodded, the man shook his head. "That plane just took off for Las Vegas. Come on, I'll help you fill out a report so they'll get your bags to your hotel by morning."

"Oh, brother," said Cathy. "There go the pajamas. And the toothpaste."

"Well, we don't need pajamas tonight," Steve wished out loud. "And we can buy toothpaste. It'll be fine."

Cathy raised an eyebrow. "If things keep going like this, we *may* need pajamas. And we may not need toothpaste."

They filled out the report and then walked to the end of Terminal One, where they waited fifteen minutes and then boarded light rail heading downtown. They sat down and looked out the window.

"See?" said Steve. "This is fun. We get to see Salt Lake at dusk. And first thing in the morning before it gets too hot, we'll go swimming in the Great Salt Lake and float because of all the salt."

Cathy looked as if she was considering, but then a middle-aged woman near them said, "Oh, you can't go in the lake right now. Too many brine flies. They don't bite, but they're sure a nuisance. You'll have to come back another time."

Cathy looked at Steve and slowly let her lip curl. Steve wondered if the hotel sold nightwear.

Getting off light rail downtown, Cathy and Steve pulled out their map and managed to find the hotel without much difficulty. On the way, they stopped in a small drugstore and Cathy didn't make any disparaging comments when Steve bought some toothpaste. That was a good sign. Then they checked in and went to their room to freshen up. Now it was time to think about dinner.

"Well, we can't go anywhere fancy with these clothes," Cathy said, but in a normal tone, not complaining. Much. "My good dress is in the suitcase."

"How hungry are you?"

"Pretty hungry. No snacks on the plane unless we paid. And I wouldn't pay on principle."

"Okay, honey." Steve smiled. "It's not like this is a five-star hotel. We can probably eat right here in our casual clothes."

"Good enough for me. Let's go."

Steve slipped his key card in his shirt pocket. They pulled the door closed behind them and walked back to the elevator. Down in the lobby, they smiled when they saw the restaurant. They waited by the hostess sign, and a pretty young woman greeted them a moment later and led them to a table. The restaurant was about a third filled, keeping the noise down.

"We've been sitting all day," Steve observed. "So why does sitting feel so good right now?"

"Because now you've got room to move."

"I'm glad we have a king-size bed." He tried to catch her eye, but Cathy was inspecting her fork as if trying to determine if it was clean enough to put in her mouth. Steve hoped he didn't see that look later.

They perused their menus for a few minutes and were ready by the time the server came to their table. "Would you like anything to drink?" she asked brightly.

"I'll have a glass of red wine…" Cathy began.

"Oh, I'm afraid we don't serve alcohol here."

"What?"

"No, ma'am. No alcohol."

"Why not? Surely, all your guests aren't Mormon."

"It's company policy."

"Isn't alcohol where restaurants make most of their money?"

"Doing the right thing is more important than making money." The young woman showed her white teeth as she smiled.

"Sheesh."

"Can I get you anything else?" the server asked.

"A Coke?" said Cathy. "Or does that have too much caffeine?"

"Yes, ma'am, we have Coke."

"I'll have a Coke, too," said Steve. The server smiled brightly again and left.

Cathy glowered at Steve from across the table. "Even in Salt Lake, I'll bet most of the hotels serve alcohol. *You* had to pick *this* hotel."

"Honey, please stop seeing the negative everywhere we go." He lowered his voice. "If we're going to make love later, it's better that I don't have any alcohol, anyway."

"And it's better that I do," Cathy whispered back.

They ate their baked chicken mostly in silence, Steve wondering if the low volume in the room was because the other couples weren't speaking to each other, either. "What do you think Sally's doing right now?" Cathy asked out of the blue.

Steve looked at her. She was still having a hard time letting go. Sally was already in her second semester of college. "Probably studying," said Steve.

"She's probably having sex with Alex," she returned.

Steve frowned. He was fine with her thinking about sex, but he wanted those thoughts to be centered on him, not their daughter. "Alex is Mormon. He's going to wait till they get married."

Cathy laughed. "Brigham Young didn't have fifty-seven children by controlling his libido."

Steve frowned. "Actually, if he had over twenty wives, fifty-seven *does* sound like self-control."

Cathy's lip curled again. "Men."

Steve began to wonder if it was already too late to salvage their marriage. He and Cathy had been growing apart for years now. It was ridiculous to think a few days in a strange city could really resolve anything.

The bright-eyed server returned to their table. "Can I get you some dessert?" she asked with a smile.

They rarely had dessert, even at home, always trying to maintain a healthy weight, and almost never when they went out, because a single slice of pie cost more than an entire cake at the grocery. But Steve grinned and put his hand on Cathy's. "Let's splurge," he said.

She stopped to really look at him, appraising rather than judgmental, and a sincere smile slowly formed on her lips. "I'll have the cheesecake," she said. "And a cup of coffee. *With* caffeine," she added. "I need to be able to stay up late tonight." She grinned back at Steve.

"Oh, I'm sorry, we don't serve coffee here."

Cathy's smile faded. "Never mind about the cheesecake."

Steve rubbed his knee against hers under the table. "Please have the cheesecake," he said. "You like milk, too."

Cathy closed her eyes and breathed deeply for a long moment. "You're right, Steve. I'm being a jerk." She turned to the server. "Cheesecake and a tall glass of milk."

"Same for me," said Steve.

Thank God neither of them was lactose intolerant.

The server walked off, and Steve risked putting his hand on Cathy's. She looked at it and didn't pull away. "Honey," he said, "pick anything, anything at all, you want to do back home, and we'll do it. If you want to attend French classes, I'll go to French class with you. If you want to study art history, we'll study art history. If you want to join a book club, I'll join a book club. If you want to start jogging, we'll jog together every day. We used to do that years ago. Whatever you want to do. We need to start having more fun together. Sally's gone. I don't want to lose you, too."

Cathy brought her hand to her mouth. "Have we lost Sally?" she asked worriedly.

"You know what I mean. We have to be there for each other." He grinned again and peeked under the table. "Your toenails *do* look good in those sandals."

Cathy turned away and looked as if she might cry. Steve was confused. Had he said something wrong?

"You're forty-eight years old," she finally said, sniffling as she turned back to him. "And *I'm* forty-six. This is exactly the time men like you turn to young women and leave their wives behind. I'm *afraid* to be too close to you. It'll hurt too much when you dump me."

Steve's mouth fell open. He'd certainly considered divorce, but not because of another woman. Only because he was so lonely with this one. "Honey," he said, "if you give up before the battle's even begun, there's no point going to battle."

She wiped her eyes. "There's going to be a battle?"

Their desserts arrived. Cathy sighed and was about to take a reluctant bite when Steve reached over with his fork and cut into her slice of pie. Cathy looked confused, and then Steve raised his fork to Cathy's lips. She smiled and took the fork into her mouth. "You are sweet sometimes," she murmured.

"I'll try to be sweet more often."

He lifted a second bite to her lips, and she smiled again.

After they paid the check, they stepped outside onto the sidewalk. The breeze was a mixture of cool and warm, as if the air couldn't decide. "We're only a few blocks from the temple," Steve said. "Let's take a stroll before heading back to the room."

"You don't want to tire yourself out," Cathy warned. "We still have some calorie-burning activities to do back there."

Steve took Cathy's hand and they began walking. It was just after 9:00, and most of the area was shut down for the evening. There were still people walking about, of course, even if Temple Square had closed. They looked through the gate and over the wall and caught glimpses of the Tabernacle roof and the temple doors. It was rather lovely, Steve reflected, notwithstanding it all being as much bunk as every other religion.

Still, Alex seemed like a nice enough young man. Sally could do worse. And it wouldn't be the end of the world to have some structure in one's life. No organization was perfect. One could always focus on the good parts and try to improve—or ignore—the rest.

Rather like one's own marriage.

Two young men in white shirts and ties approached. Steve wasn't in the mood to talk religion right before taking Cathy back to their room to ravish her, but he did want to be polite. "Isn't it time you guys turned in for the night?" he asked with a smile.

One of the young men raised his hand and pointed something at them. Steve looked down. It was a gun.

"What the—?"

"Give me your wallet," said the young man with the gun.

"And give me your purse," the other man ordered Cathy.

"But…but…" Cathy spluttered.

"You dweebs always let us get close when we wear these outfits." The man with the gun laughed. "Now give it up!" He shoved the gun into Steve's ribs. Steve pulled out his wallet, and Cathy handed over her purse. Why had she even brought her purse when they were just going down to the hotel lobby? Now they had nothing.

The young men turned and ran away. Steve didn't even shout.

Cathy took Steve's hand gently, putting her head on his shoulder. "Let's go back to the hotel before someone steals our shoes," she said softly.

They walked back slowly, not even telling anyone at the front desk what had happened. They could do that later. They took the elevator to their room, closed the door without turning on the lights, and opened the drapes to look out over Temple Square. "Take off everything but your sandals," Steve said quietly.

"Oh, darling!"

Steve licked Cathy's toes and then pushed her up against the window, entering her as he looked at the temple spires twinkling in the background. He stared at the angel's long, glistening horn and kissed Cathy on the lips. She thrust her tongue deep into his throat. Steve would buy Cathy a new pair of shoes while they were in Salt Lake. Something to remember this night and their revitalized commitment to one another. Maybe something with a stiletto.

She could wear them when they renewed their vows on Main Street Plaza tomorrow night.

Books by Johnny Townsend

Thanks for reading! If you enjoyed this book, could you please take a few minutes to write a review online? Reviews are helpful both to me as an author and to other readers, so we'd all sincerely appreciate your writing one! And if you did enjoy the book, here are some others I've written you might want to look up:

Mormon Underwear

Sex among the Saints

Zombies for Jesus

A Gay Mormon Missionary in Pompeii

The Golem of Rabbi Loew

Mormon Fairy Tales

Marginal Mormons

Mormon Bullies

The Mormon Victorian Society

Dragons of the Book of Mormon

Gayrabian Nights

Lying for the Lord

Despots of Deseret

Missionaries Make the Best Companions

Invasion of the Spirit Snatchers

The Washing of Brains

Interview with a Mission President

Weeping, Wailing, and Gnashing of Teeth

Behind the Bishop's Door

The Moat around Zion

The Last Days Linger

Mormon Madness

Human Compassion for Beginners

Dead Mankind Walking

Breaking the Promise of the Promised Land

I Will, Through the Veil

Am I My Planet's Keeper?

Have Your Cum and Eat It, Too

Strangers with Benefits

Constructing Equity

Wake Up and Smell the Missionaries

Racism by Proxy

Orgy at the STD Clinic

Life Is Better with Love

Please Evacuate

Recommended Daily Humanity

The Camper Killings

Kinky Quilts: Patchwork Designs for Gay Men

Inferno in the French Quarter: The UpStairs Lounge Fire

Latter-Gay Saints: An Anthology of Gay Mormon Fiction (co-editor)

Available from your favorite online or neighborhood bookstore.

Wondering what some of those other books are about? Read on!

Invasion of the Spirit Snatchers

During the Apocalypse, a group of Mormon survivors in Hurricane, Utah gather in the home of the Relief Society president, telling stories to pass the time as they ration their food storage and await the Second Coming. But this is no ordinary group of Mormons—or perhaps it is. They are the faithful, feminist, gay, apostate, and repentant, all working together to help each other through the darkest days any of them have yet seen.

Gayrabian Nights

Gayrabian Nights is a twist on the well-known classic, *1001 Arabian Nights*, in which Scheherazade, under the threat of death if she ceases to captivate King Shahryar's attention, enchants him through a series of mysterious, adventurous, and romantic tales.

In this variation, a male escort, invited to the hotel room of a closeted, homophobic Mormon senator, learns that the man is poised to vote on a piece of anti-gay legislation the following morning. To prevent him from sleeping, so that the exhausted senator will miss casting his vote on the Senate floor, the escort entertains him with stories of homophobia, celibacy, mixed orientation marriages, reparative therapy, coming out, first love, gay marriage, and long-term successful gay relationships. The escort crafts the stories to give the senator a crash course in gay culture and sensibilities, hoping to bring the man closer to accepting his own sexual orientation.

Inferno in the French Quarter: The UpStairs Lounge Fire

On Gay Pride Day in 1973, someone set the entrance to a French Quarter gay bar on fire. In the terrible inferno that followed, thirty-two people lost their lives, including a third of the local congregation of the Metropolitan Community Church, their pastor burning to death halfway out a second-story window as he tried to claw his way to freedom. A mother who'd gone to the bar with her two gay sons died alongside them. A man who'd helped his friend escape first was found dead near the fire escape. Two children waited outside a movie theater across town for a father and step-father who would never pick them up. During this era of rampant homophobia, several families refused to claim the bodies, and many churches refused to bury the dead. Author Johnny Townsend pored through old records and tracked down survivors of the fire as well as relatives and friends of those killed to compile this fascinating account of a forgotten moment in gay history.

A Gay Mormon Missionary in Pompeii

What is a gay Mormon missionary doing in Italy? He is trying to save his own soul as well as the souls of others. In these tales chronicling the two-year mission of Robert Anderson, we see a young man tormented by his inability to be the man the Church says he should be. In addition to his personal hell, Anderson faces a major earthquake, organized crime, a serious bus accident, and much more. He copes with horrendous mission leaders and his own suicidal tendencies. But one day, he meets another missionary who loves him, and his world changes forever.

Missionaries Make the Best Companions

What lies behind the freshly scrubbed façades of the Mormon missionaries we see about town? In these stories, an ex-Mormon tries to seduce a faithful elder by showing him increasingly suggestive movies. A sister missionary fulfills her community service requirement by babysitting for a prostitute. Two elders break their mission rules by venturing into the forbidden French Quarter. A senior missionary couple try to reactivate lapsed members while their own family falls apart back home. A young man hopes that serving a second full-time mission will lead him up the Church hierarchy. Two bored missionaries decide to make a little extra money moonlighting in a male stripper club. Two frustrated elders find an acceptable way to masturbate—by donating to a Fertility Clinic. A lonely man searches for the favorite companion he hasn't seen in thirty years.

The Golem of Rabbi Loew

Jacob and Esau Cohen are the closest of brothers. In fact, they're lovers. A doctor tries to combine canine genes with those of Jews, to improve their chances of surviving a hostile world. A Talmudic scholar dates an escort. A scientist tries to develop the "God spot" in the brains of his patients in order to create a messiah. The Golem of Prague is really Rabbi Loew's secret lover. While some of the Jews in Townsend's book are Orthodox, this collection of Jewish stories most certainly is not.

The Last Days Linger

The scriptures tell us that in the Last Days, wickedness will increase upon the Earth. When leaders of the Mormon Church see a rise in the number of gay members, they believe the end is upon them. But while "wickedness never was happiness," it begins to appear that wickedness can sometimes be divine. At least, the stories here suggest that religious proscriptions condemning homosexuality have it all wrong. While gay Mormons may be no closer to perfection than anyone else, they're no further from it, either. And sometimes, being gay provides just the right ingredient to create saints—as flawed as God himself.

Mormon Madness

Mental illness can strike the faithful as easily as anyone else. But often religious doctrine and practice exacerbate rather than alleviate these problems. From schizophrenia to obsessive-compulsive disorder, from persecution complex to sexual dysfunction, autism to dissociative identity disorder, Mormons must cope with their mental as well as their spiritual health on a daily basis.

Am I My Planet's Keeper?

Global Warming. Climate Change. Climate Crisis. Climate Emergency. Whatever label we use, we are facing one of the greatest challenges to the survival of life as we know it.

But while addressing greenhouse gases is perhaps our most urgent need, it's not our only task. We must also address toxic waste, pollution, habitat destruction, and our other contributions to the world's sixth mass extinction event.

In order to do that, we must simultaneously address the unmet human needs that keep us distracted from deeper engagement in stabilizing our climate: moderating economic inequality, guaranteeing healthcare to all, and ensuring education for everyone.

And to accomplish *that*, we must unite to combat the monied forces that use fear, prejudice, and misinformation to manipulate us.

It's a daunting task. But success is our only option.

Wake Up and Smell the Missionaries

Two Mormon missionaries in Italy discover they share the same rare ability—both can emit pheromones on demand. At first, they playfully compete in the hills of Frascati to see who can tempt "investigators" most. But soon they're targeting each other non-stop.

Can two immature young men learn to control their "superpower" to live a normal life…and develop genuine love? Even as their relationship is threatened by the attentions of another man?

They seem just on the verge of success when a massive earthquake leaves them trapped under the rubble of their apartment in Castellammare.

With night falling and temperatures dropping, can they dig themselves out in time to save themselves? And will their injuries destroy the ability that brought them together in the first place?

Orgy at the STD Clinic

Todd Tillotson is struggling to move on after his husband is killed in a hit and run attack a year earlier during a Black Lives Matter protest in Seattle.

In this novel set entirely on public transportation, we watch as Todd, isolated throughout the pandemic, battles desperation in his attempt to safely reconnect with the world.

Will he find love again, even casual friendship, or will he simply end up another crazy old man on the bus?

Things don't look good until a man whose face he can't even see sits down beside him despite the raging variants.

And asks him a question that will change his life.

Please Evacuate

A gay, partygoing New Yorker unconcerned about the future or the unsustainability of capitalism is hit by a truck and thrust into a straight man's body half a continent away. As Hunter tries to figure out what's happening, he's caught up in another disaster, a wildfire sweeping through a Colorado community, the flames overtaking him and several schoolchildren as they flee.

When he awakens, Hunter finds himself in the body of yet another man, this time in northern Italy, a former missionary about to marry a young Mormon woman. Still piecing together this new reality, and beginning to embrace his latest identity, Hunter fights for his life in a devastating flash flood along with his wife *and* his new husband.

He's an aging worker in drought-stricken Texas, a nurse at an assisted living facility in the direct path of a hurricane, an advocate for the unhoused during a freak Seattle blizzard.

We watch as Hunter is plunged into life after life, finally recognizing the futility of only looking out for #1 and understanding the part he must play in addressing the global climate crisis...if he ever gets another chance.

Recommended Daily Humanity

A checklist of human rights must include basic housing, universal healthcare, equitable funding for public schools, and tuition-free college and vocational training.

In addition to the basics, though, we need much more to fully thrive. Subsidized childcare, universal pre-K, a universal basic income, subsidized high-speed internet, net neutrality, fare-free public transit (plus *more* public transit), and medically assisted death for the terminally ill who want it.

None of this will matter, though, if we neglect to address the rapidly worsening climate crisis.

Sound expensive? It is.

But not as expensive as refusing to implement these changes. The cost of climate disasters each year has grown to staggering figures. And the cost of social and political upheaval from not meeting the needs of suffering workers, families, and individuals may surpass even that.

It's best we understand that the vast sums required to enact meaningful change are an investment which will pay off not only in some indeterminate future but in fact almost immediately. And without these adjustments to our lifestyles and values, there may very well not be a future capable of sustaining freedom and democracy...or even civilization itself.

The Camper Killings

When a homeless man is found murdered a few blocks from Morgan Beylerian's house in south Seattle, everyone seems to consider the body just so much additional trash to be cleared from the neighborhood. But Morgan liked the guy. They used to chat when Morgan brought Nick groceries once a week.

And the brutal way the man was killed reminds Morgan of their shared Mormon heritage, back when the faithful agreed to have their throats slit if they ever revealed temple secrets.

Did Nick's former wife take action when her ex-husband refused to grant a temple divorce? Did his murder have something to do with the public accusations that brought an end to his promising career?

Morgan does his best to investigate when no one else seems to care, but it isn't easy as a man living paycheck to paycheck himself, only able to pursue his investigation via public transit.

As he continues his search for the killer, Morgan's friends withdraw and his husband threatens to leave. When another homeless man is killed and Morgan is accused of the crime, things look even bleaker.

But his troubles aren't over yet.

Will Morgan find the killer before the killer finds him?

What Readers Have Said

Townsend's stories are "a gay *Portnoy's Complaint* of Mormonism. Salacious, sweet, sad, insightful, insulting, religiously ethnic, quirky-faithful, and funny."

D. Michael Quinn, author of *The Mormon Hierarchy: Origins of Power*

"Told from a believably conversational first-person perspective, [*A Gay Mormon Missionary in Pompeii*'s] novelistic focus on Anderson's journey to thoughtful self-acceptance allows for greater character development than often seen in short stories, which makes this well-paced work rich and satisfying, and one of Townsend's strongest. An extremely important contribution to the field of Mormon fiction." Named to Kirkus Reviews' Best of 2011.

Kirkus Reviews

"The thirteen stories in *Mormon Underwear* capture this struggle [between Mormonism and homosexuality] with humor, sadness, insight, and sometimes shocking details....*Mormon Underwear* provides compelling stories, literally from the inside-out."

Niki D'Andrea, *Phoenix New Times*

"Townsend's lively writing style and engaging characters [in *Zombies for Jesus*] make for stories which force us to wake up, smell the (prohibited) coffee, and review our attitudes with regard to reading dogma so doggedly. These are tales which revel in the individual tics and quirks which make us human, Mormon or not, gay or not…"

A.J. Kirby, *The Short Review*

"The Rift," from *A Gay Mormon Missionary in Pompeii*, is a "fascinating tale of an untenable situation…a *tour de force*."

David Lenson, editor, *The Massachusetts Review*

"Pronouncing the Apostrophe," from *The Golem of Rabbi Loew*, is "quiet and revealing, an intriguing tale…"

Sima Rabinowitz, Literary Magazine Review, *NewPages.com*

The Circumcision of God is "a collection of short stories that consider the imperfect, silenced majority of Mormons, who may in fact be [the Church's] best hope….[The book leaves] readers regretting the church's willingness to marginalize those who best exemplify its ideals: those who love fiercely despite all obstacles, who brave challenges at great personal risk and who always choose the hard, higher road."

Kirkus Reviews

In *Mormon Fairy Tales*, Johnny Townsend displays "both a wicked sense of irony and a deep well of compassion."

Kel Munger, *Sacramento News and Review*

Zombies for Jesus is "eerie, erotic, and magical."

Publishers Weekly

"While [Townsend's] many touching vignettes draw deeply from Mormon mythology, history, spirituality and culture, [*Mormon Fairy Tales*] is neither a gaudy act of proselytism nor angry protest literature from an ex-believer. Like all good fiction, his stories are simply about the joys, the hopes and the sorrows of people."

Kirkus Reviews

"In *Inferno in the French Quarter* author Johnny Townsend restores this tragic event [the UpStairs Lounge fire] to its proper place in LGBT history and reminds us that the victims of the blaze were not just 'statistics,' but real people with real lives, families, and friends."

Jesse Monteagudo, *The Bilerico Project*

In *Inferno in the French Quarter*, "Townsend's heart-rending descriptions of the victims…seem to [make them] come alive once more."

Kit Van Cleave, *OutSmart Magazine*

Marginal Mormons is "an irreverent, honest look at life outside the mainstream Mormon Church….Throughout his musings on sin and forgiveness, Townsend beautifully demonstrates his characters' internal, perhaps irreconcilable struggles….Rather than anger and disdain, he offers an honest portrayal of people searching for meaning and community in their lives, regardless of their life choices or secrets." Named to Kirkus Reviews' Best of 2012.

Kirkus Reviews

The stories in *The Mormon Victorian Society* "register the new openness and confidence of gay life in the age of same-sex marriage….What hasn't changed is Townsend's wry, conversational prose, his subtle evocations of character and social dynamics, and his deadpan humor. His warm empathy still glows in this intimate yet clear-eyed engagement with Mormon theology and folkways. Funny, shrewd and finely wrought dissections of the awkward contradictions—and surprising harmonies—between conscience and desire." Named to Kirkus Reviews' Best of 2013.

Kirkus Reviews

"This collection of short stories [*The Mormon Victorian Society*] featuring gay Mormon characters slammed [me] in the face from the first page, wrestled my heart and mind to the floor, and left me panting and wanting more by the end. Johnny Townsend has created so many memorable characters in such few pages. I went weeks thinking about this book. It truly touched me."

Tom Webb, *A Bear on Books*

Dragons of the Book of Mormon is an "entertaining collection....Townsend's prose is sharp, clear, and easy to read, and his characters are well rendered..."

Publishers Weekly

"The pre-eminent documenter of alternative Mormon lifestyles...Townsend has a deep understanding of his characters, and his limpid prose, dry humor and well-grounded (occasionally magical) realism make their spiritual conundrums both compelling and entertaining. [*Dragons of the Book of Mormon* is] [a]nother of Townsend's critical but affectionate and absorbing tours of Mormon discontent." Named to Kirkus Reviews' Best of 2014.

Kirkus Reviews

In *Gayrabian Nights*, "Townsend's prose is always limpid and evocative, and…he finds real drama and emotional depth in the most ordinary of lives."

Kirkus Reviews

Gayrabian Nights is a "complex revelation of how seriously soul damaging the denial of the true self can be."

Ryan Rhodes, author of *Free Electricity*

Gayrabian Nights "was easily the most original book I've read all year. Funny, touching, topical, and thoroughly enjoyable."

Rainbow Awards

Lying for the Lord is "one of the most gripping books that I've picked up for quite a while. I love the author's writing style, alternately cynical, humorous, biting, scathing, poignant, and touching…. This is the third book of his that I've read, and all are equally engaging. These are stories that need to be told, and the author does it in just the right way."

Heidi Alsop, *Ex-Mormon Foundation Board Member*

In *Lying for the Lord*, Townsend "gets under the skin of his characters to reveal their complexity and conflicts....shrewd, evocative [and] wryly humorous."

Kirkus Reviews

In *Missionaries Make the Best Companions*, "the author treats the clash between religious dogma and liberal humanism with vivid realism, sly humor, and subtle feeling as his characters try to figure out their true missions in life. Another of Townsend's rich dissections of Mormon failures and uncertainties..." Named to Kirkus Reviews' Best of 2015.

Kirkus Reviews

In *Invasion of the Spirit Snatchers*, "Townsend, a confident and practiced storyteller, skewers the hypocrisies and eccentricities of his characters with precision and affection. The outlandish framing narrative is the most consistent source of shock and humor, but the stories do much to ground the reader in the world—or former world—of the characters....A funny, charming tale about a group of Mormons facing the end of the world."

Kirkus Reviews

"Townsend's collection [*The Washing of Brains*] once again displays his limpid, naturalistic prose, skillful narrative chops, and his subtle insights into psychology...Well-crafted dispatches on the clash between religion and self-fulfillment..."

Kirkus Reviews

"While the author is generally at his best when working as a satirist, there are some fine, understated touches in these tales [*The Last Days Linger*] that will likely affect readers in subtle ways….readers should come away impressed by the deep empathy he shows for all his characters—even the homophobic ones."

Kirkus Reviews

"Written in a conversational style that often uses stories and personal anecdotes to reveal larger truths, this immensely approachable book [*Racism by Proxy*] skillfully serves its intended audience of White readers grappling with complex questions regarding race, history, and identity. The author's frequent references to the Church of Jesus Christ of Latter-day Saints may be too niche for readers unfamiliar with its idiosyncrasies, but Townsend generally strikes a perfect balance of humor, introspection, and reasoned arguments that will engage even skeptical readers."

Kirkus Reviews

Orgy at the STD Clinic portrays "an all-too real scenario that Townsend skewers to wincingly accurate proportions…[with] instant classic moments courtesy of his punchy, sassy, sexy lead character…"

Jim Piechota, *Bay Area Reporter*

Orgy at the STD Clinic is "…a triumph of humane sensibility. A richly textured saga that brilliantly captures the fraying social fabric of contemporary life." Named to Kirkus Reviews' Best Indie Books of 2022.

Kirkus Reviews

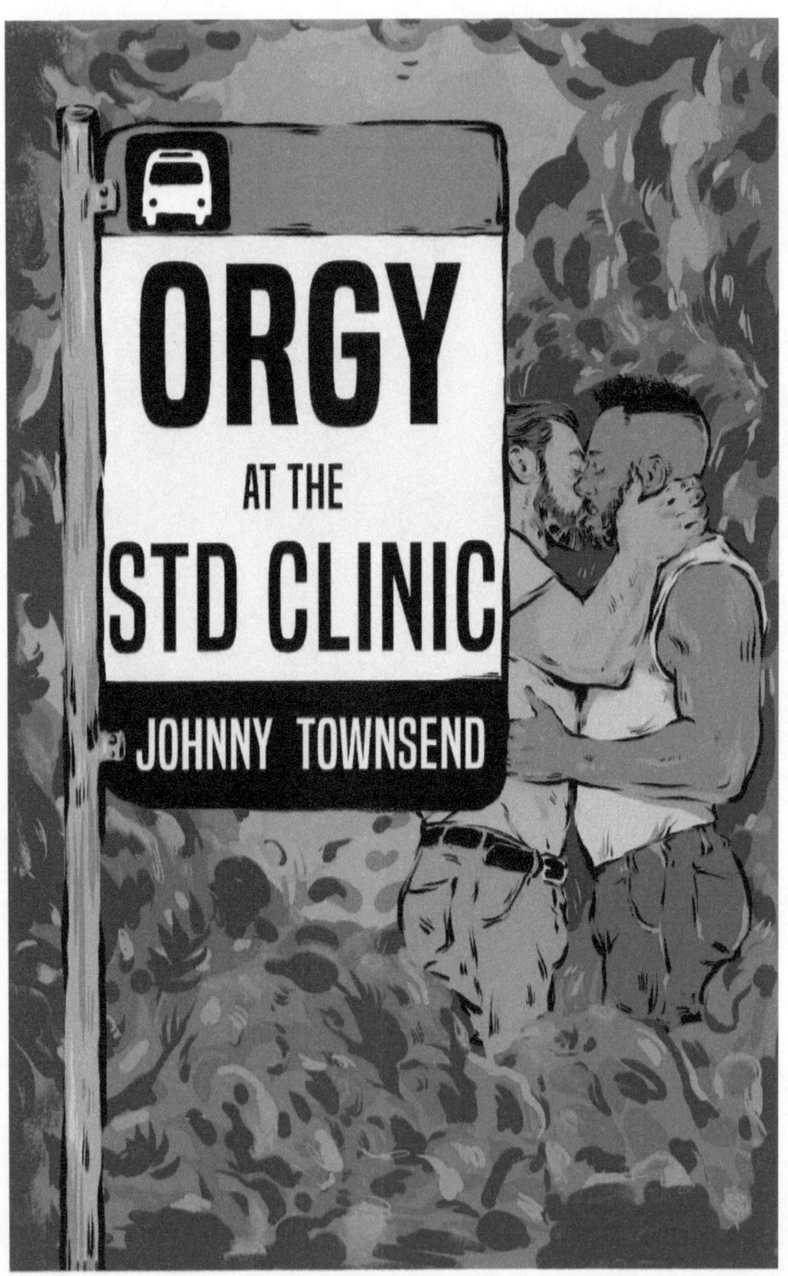

ORGY
AT THE
STD CLINIC
JOHNNY TOWNSEND

HAVE
YOUR CUM
AND
EAT IT, TOO
JOHNNY TOWNSEND